APPL

Paula's success in her final nursing exam co-
incides with her fiancé abruptly breaking off their
engagement. To recover from the blow, she joins
the Tasmanian Tourist Nursing Service—and
finds a new life, and a new love.

APPLE ISLAND

BY

GLADYS FULLBROOK

MILLS & BOON LIMITED
London · Sydney · Toronto

First published in Great Britain 1962
by Mills & Boon Limited, 15-16 Brook's Mews,
London W1A 1DR

This edition 1982
© Gladys Fullbrook 1962

Australian copyright 1982
Philippine copyright 1982

ISBN 0 263 73794 2

03/0282

Set in 10 on 10½pt Times Roman

Photoset by Rowland Phototypesetting Ltd.,
Bury St Edmunds, Suffolk.
Made and printed in Great Britain by
Richard Clay (The Chaucer Press) Ltd.,
Bungay, Suffolk

CHAPTER ONE

ROSALIND LANE sat on the side of her bed reading a letter. She did not look up when the door opened. It would be Paula, she knew.

'Letter from Mother,' she said. 'She wants us to go home this weekend. They're all thrilled at the news, and Daddy suggests that we celebrate with a party on Saturday night.' She became conscious all at once of the unnatural silence in the room and looked up in mild surprise. Then, 'Paula!' she said sharply, at the sight of the other girl's face. 'What's the matter? Are you ill?'

Paula Bruce's face was pale and drawn. She looked at Rosalind in a dazed kind of way and moved slowly over to the dressing table. With her back to the other girl she said in a jerky dull voice quite unlike her own, 'It's—Bob.'

There was a short silence, then Rosalind said quietly, 'What about him, Paula?'

Her companion swallowed almost audibly, then, in a muffled voice she said, 'He's married,' and began to laugh, a discordant, high-pitched laugh which changed suddenly to a harsh sobbing.

Rosalind jumped up, crossed the room swiftly and took Paula by the shoulders. 'Stop it,' she said. 'Stop it, Paula, before someone hears you,' and shook her violently.

After a few more convulsive sobs, Paula Bruce stopped as suddenly as she had started. Tears zig-zagged down her cheeks, and her mouth hung slack and trembling. 'All right, Ross,' she gulped, 'you can stop manhandling me. I'm O.K. now.'

'Come and sit down,' Rosalind said gently, leading her to the bed. 'Now tell me all about it.'

Paula slumped heavily down. She made an impatient

effort at self-control, then looked at Rosalind out of bewildered, unhappy eyes.

'Sorry,' she muttered abruptly, 'but—I had a letter, too.' There was a pause while Rosalind waited for her to go on. 'He—he met a girl out there.' She looked down at her clenched hands. 'And—and he's not coming back to England. It's—all over.' The last words seemed to hang in the air with a kind of bleak finality.

'Oh, Paula!' Rosalind began, but the other girl rose quickly to her feet and crossed to the window.

'I don't want to talk about it—yet,' she said in a hard little voice. Rosalind did not follow her. She sensed that Paula was fighting hard for composure and knew that she would do it better alone.

'I'm sorry, Paula,' she said. 'It's all one can say, isn't it? But let me say just one thing. Don't take it too hard, and don't let it get you down.' She paused, and the silence was broken only by the other girl's quick breathing. Then Rosalind's voice began again. 'You've done so well in all your exams. We all know what Sister Tutor thinks of you; she says you're a born nurse. Why, Paula, the whole world is open to you. I never did think Bob Shaw was the right man for you, and neither did Mummy and Daddy. You'll meet someone else, you'll see. You're so pretty, and—'

'Perhaps,' Paula interrupted roughly. She continued to stare out of the window, then swung round to face her friend. 'But at present I feel I'll never trust another man as long as I live.' Rosalind reached over for a cigarette.

'You feel like that now, of course,' she said, deliberately pitching her voice to a light and commonplace note, 'but—well, you're only twenty-three, you know.'

'I know,' Paula said, 'but—I trusted Bob so completely, and—and—' her voice broke, and suddenly her head went down into her arms. Rosalind crossed the room and silently put both arms round her. She held Paula without saying a word till the hard sobs had subsided and there was nothing but an exhausted emptiness in the room. Presently Paula raised her head and looked at Rosalind with a twisted little grin. 'Well, that's that,' she said. 'A chapter of my life is over, and now I must gather up the pieces, I suppose.'

Rosalind gave her one last quick hug, then said in a determinedly cheerful voice, 'That's better. Now, you're coming with me for the weekend, aren't you? The parents are dying to congratulate us on our exam results and hear all the news. You will come, Paula—please?'

'No, I don't think so, Ross,' Paula said slowly. She was standing at the wash-bowl now, dabbing her face with a face-cloth. 'I—guess I'd like these next two days to,' she picked up the towel, 'get my bearings, sort of thing.' She peered into the mirror, then turned to look at Rosalind. 'I'm not going to mope around, Ross, but I must get myself sorted out. You understand?'

'Yes, of course, and if that's what you want—O.K. Now, let's doll ourselves up and go out and have a meal, shall we? Something wildly extravagant to celebrate the beginning of our nursing careers. Just think, Paula, we could go almost anywhere. Why, the very thought of it makes me light-headed. Come on, let's go.'

The two girls had just completed their nursing training, and had had the news of their final success only the day before. Paula was an orphan, her parents having been killed in an accident. She had been staying with Rosalind's family in Somerset; and when the tragedy occurred the warm-hearted farmer and his wife adopted the lonely little girl. Paula and Rosalind had been like sisters from the first, and were almost inseparable. They had gone together as student nurses to St Just's Hospital, and had kept pace with each other till the final examination. And now the day for which they had both worked so hard had come. The day on which they were qualified to put the coveted letters, S.R.N., S.C.M. after their names.

Paula had met Bob Shaw, a radio officer in the Merchant Navy, at a hospital dance. There had been a whirlwind courtship, and within a month the two were engaged. Rosalind and her parents had met Bob, of course, and though little was said, Paula knew that they were not impressed by her choice. But it made no difference to her. Bob was everything she had ever dreamed of in a lover. He had wanted Paula to give up nursing and marry him at once. But, though she was thrilled, Paula was not willing to do this. She loved her work and had set her heart on qualifying. She reminded Bob that she had less than a year to do; and as he was already signed up for a six-months' voyage on a tanker, it seemed foolish not to carry on for such a short time more. Paula won her point, and rather reluctantly Bob gave in.

All that was five months ago; and though Paula had not seen him for the last four months, his letter had given no indication of a change of heart. True, he had not mentioned marriage lately, but then neither had Paula. Her work, and studying for her finals, had completely filled her thoughts—and she was so sure of Bob. Now she wondered bleakly if she had been too prudent and cautious; whether she should have married Bob when he asked her. Well, Paula shrugged her shoulders, it's too late now, she reminded herself. By the time you get this I shall be married, he had said in the letter.

Paula had seen Rosalind off for the weekend, and now she was back in her room in the Nurses' Hostel. It was mid-morning, and very quiet. She sat down, hands idle in her lap, and feeling curiously empty. For the last year Paula's life had revolved round Bob. Beyond that she had not really gone. But now? Well, she'd got her nursing and midwifery qualifications, at any rate. She'd have to build now from there. For a moment the future stretched before her, flat and empty; but only for a moment. Don't be a fool, she told herself. This sort of thing is happening all the time to someone—and they get over it. Just as you will. You're not the only one by any means. Though she had said to Rosalind that she could never trust another man, Paula knew that this feeling would not last. She was a normal girl, and looked forward to love, marriage and children. No, it was just that, at present, she could not envisage a future with any other man but Bob Shaw.

Paula rose and wandered aimlessly over to the dressing table. She looked at herself in the mirror and was half surprised to see that this sudden and shattering blow she had received had left no mark on her face. Her eyes were as clear as hazel, her hair as black, and her cheeks as pink and smooth as ever. Bob used to say that she looked like apple-blossom. And at the sudden swift thought, and the realisation that he would never say it to her again, Paula's head went down into her hands and the forlorn tears flowed unchecked. But after a moment she raised her head and pushed the cloudy hair impatiently from her damp brow. She got out a handkerchief, shook herself, and began restlessly to pace the room. Coming again to the mirror, she paused and stared again at her reflection.

'You've got to accept it,' she said aloud. Somehow, speaking the words helped to make it real. 'It's all finished; you're all washed up, Paula Bruce. There's no Bob any more.' Her chin quivered as for a moment a mental picture flashed before her. Bob—gay, smiling, and loving—as she had last seen him. But with an effort Paula controlled herself and went on: 'You're on your own now, and—' what was it Rosalind had said? Yes. 'The whole wide world is open to you.' That's right, Paula thought, with the first faint lifting of the heart, the whole world. All right, then, where do I go from here?

And then she remembered, with a stab of remorse, that in the days before she had met Bob, she and Rosalind had had many exciting plans for the time when they would be fully qualified. They would go here, there, and everywhere. Together they had explored the possibilities of a nursing career in other lands.

But when Paula became engaged to Bob, Rosalind and the plans had slipped quietly into the background. Paula's future plans must necessarily depend on Bob now, and as time went on Rosalind spoke less and less of her own future. She was still interested in nursing over-seas, Paula knew, but did not seem to have settled on any particular place. Paula realised now how very un-selfish her friend had been. She had never once spoken of her own disappointment, except to say that of course it was quite natural that Paula should fall in love and want to marry. Well, Paula thought, she was back where she started. She and Rosalind could still do what they had originally planned. But perhaps Ross had ideas of her own, ideas which could not include her friend. But somehow Paula thought not. Rosalind would have said something, she was sure.

Paula wandered over to her bed and sat down. She had promised Rosalind that she would not mope while she was away, and she did not intend to do so. Firmly now she banished thoughts of Bob, and turned her atten-tion to what she was going to do now. Well, what have I got to face the world with? she asked herself. I've got youth, health, my share of good looks, *and* my double certificate. That's pretty good to go on with. And on the debit side, what? A disappointment in love. Well, she wasn't going to let that get her down. She would stop thinking about Bob and all that he had meant in her life and look forward instead to the future. Paula had a miserable suspicion that it was not going to be as easy as all that; but she pushed the thought from her and deter-mined to start right now. Jumping to her feet, she marched resolutely to the mirror and stared into her own face.

'Wash and tidy yourself up,' she said to it. 'Put on some make-up, and your best suit, and then go out—anywhere.'

Paula had one more moment of weakness when, searching for the room key in her handbag, she came across a snapshot of Bob, gay and handsome, with "To my darling Paula, with all my love, Bob" scrawled at the bottom of it. She looked at it for a moment with un-steady lips, then quickly thrust it again into the depths of the bag. Not yet could Paula bring herself to tear it up and throw it into the waste-paper basket.

She blinked away a few tears, drew a comb through her hair, and powdered her face. Then, pulling on her coat, Paula picked up her gloves and handbag and went quickly out of the room.

On Sunday night Rosalind returned. 'Hello, love,' she greeted Paula. 'Dad and Mum send their love.' She hung up her coat, watching Paula covertly from the corner of her eye. She was relieved to see that she was composed and looked reasonably cheerful. 'What have you been doing over the weekend?'

'Oh, hello Ross. I've been—quite busy.' Rosalind thought she detected an undertone of excitement in Paula's voice. She looked her surprise, then said, 'Good. Let's get into bed, and then we can swop news. I'll go and collect two cups of coffee.' She vanished on the words and returned in a few minutes with the coffee and some biscuits. Paula was already in bed. Rosalind sat on the side of hers and kicked off her shoes. She saw that Paula really had something to tell her, and rapidly got on with the job of undressing.

'Well, come on, Paula,' she said presently, settling herself against the pillows, 'shoot. I can see you've been up to something. Is it something to do with future plans?' She hesitated, then added, 'I told Mummy, Paula. She's anxious about you. I'm afraid she's worrying because you didn't come down with me.'

'Oh, I'm sorry, Ross.' Paula's voice was apologetic. 'It was selfish of me not to think of her. I'll write tomorrow, and go down next time. I'm glad you told her. But she need not worry. I did a lot of sorting out this weekend, and—I think I know what I'm going to do.'

Rosalind sat up straight in bed and put down her cup. She stared at Paula. 'What do you mean?' she said, and waited.

'As a matter of fact, I've already done it. At least, I've filled in the papers.' Paula's voice was almost casual, but it did not deceive Rosalind.

'Papers!' she echoed. 'What papers?' and twisted over sideways in her bed.

'I'm going to join the Tasmanian Tourist Nursing Service,' Paula said calmly, and took a sip of her coffee.

'Tasmania!' Rosalind said, staring. 'Why, that's the place we often talked about. But this—what did you call it, Tourist Nursing Service? I never heard of it.'

Paula giggled suddenly. 'If you could only see your face,' she remarked. 'Well, anyway, I was walking down the Strand,' she continued, 'and right at the top I saw them—the pictures. They seemed to call me. It was just as if a door was being opened. So I went in, and Ross, I think I really made up my mind on the spot.'

'But I never heard of it,' Rosalind said again. 'This Tourist Nursing Service, I mean.'

'Neither had I till I went in,' Paula said, laughing now. 'But it sounds terribly interesting, Ross. There was such a nice girl in the office. She told me there are vacancies out there for double-certificated nurses, and one can register *here* for their Nursing Service. There's a Government arrangement, apparently. So you see, you can apply here for a job out there. You can also get an assisted passage, and have an interview on arrival.' Paula was quite breathless by now, and her eyes were shining.

'So you haven't actually joined this—Tourist Service yet?' Rosalind asked, watching her.

'Well, not exactly. You see, I've got to have the interview. The girl in the office told me that the Matron of the Centre happens to be in London at present combining holidays with business, *and* she is interviewing applicants.'

'And you're having an interview?' Rosalind's eyes were bright with anticipation.

'Yes, tomorrow. Of course I don't know if I shall be accepted, but—'

'Of course you'll be accepted,' Rosalind interrupted. 'With your certificates, *and* your report from Matron— why, it's in the bag. Tell me more about it, Paula,' and she hugged her knees in suspense. 'What exactly does it do?'

'Well,' Paula began, then paused to drain her cup, 'it's a service composed of Sisters, who go from one hospital to another wherever they are needed. You know, when any of them are short-staffed then the Tourist Nursing Service sends someone. It seems to me a wonderful way to get a wide and varied experience of nursing, combined with travel in a lovely country. The girl at the office comes from Tasmania and she told me all about it; and the pictures look most glamorous. They call it Apple Island.'

'Sounds marvellous,' Rosalind agreed, happy to see that Paula was already putting the past behind her and reaching out to a new life. 'Do they want many, d'you know?'

'The girl said there are always vacancies for double-certificated nurses,' Paula said, and waited breathlessly. Rosalind looked at her.

'Well, how about me coming too?' she asked. 'It seems—' but she never finished the sentence. For Paula leapt out of bed and flung herself upon her friend.

'Oh, Ross!' she said. 'I hoped you'd say that, but I felt I ought not to suggest it, after—after, well, we haven't talked much lately about the future, and—I thought you might have plans of your own, and it wouldn't be fair, but, oh, it'll be marvellous to do it together, and—'

'Just a minute,' Rosalind said, laughing. 'Aren't we both counting our chickens, especially me? But if you go—well, so do I if they'll take me.'

'The girl there said they do want qualified nurses badly,' Paula said, her cheeks rosy with excitement. 'When will you go about it, Ross?'

'I'll get the papers tomorrow. I'm off duty in the morning.'

'No need. I got them for you,' Paula said calmly. 'You can fill them in before you go.' She coughed. 'I fixed up an interview for you, too.' Rosalind stared at her.

'Well!' she said, and burst out laughing, then reached

over for the papers Paula was holding out. 'How did you know I'd want to?' she asked.

Paula smiled. 'I didn't,' she said. 'I just hoped you would; and it saves time, doesn't it?'

Rosalind gave a long sigh of satisfaction. 'Oh, Paula! It's like old times, isn't it?' she said, scanning the papers eagerly.

'Ross, you don't think the parents will mind—and blame me, do you?' There was a note of anxiety in Paula's voice.

'Not a bit of it,' Rosalind replied. 'As you know, Mummy loves travel, even if it's only as far as Weston-super-Mare. And she's always encouraged me to get around and see places. Dad may not be so keen. How long is this job for?'

'Well,' Paula said, 'supposing we're accepted, and assisted passages are granted, we'd be in it for two years to begin with. After that—well, I suppose it would be up to us.'

Rosalind looked thoughtful. 'It sounds fine,' she said after a short pause, 'but—this two years. Does that mean we'd have to stay in the jobs, even if, suppose, one of us, or both, wanted to marry?'

Paula laughed shortly. 'I'm not likely to,' she said. 'But anyway, you can set your mind at rest on that point. The two years really refers to the assisted passages. We'd be expected to remain in the country for that length of time. But for the jobs, we'd be free to change them if we wished. I asked about that, Ross.' Rosalind smiled at her and folded the papers.

'Right,' she said, 'then everything's just "bonzer" as I believe they call it out there. You're certainly not having this all to yourself, Paula Bruce.'

The latter smiled. 'As a matter of fact,' she said, 'I felt almost certain that it would be just up your street. Well, I suppose we'd better get some sleep.' She stretched and slid down between the sheets. 'There are thousands of things to do before we pack and move out at the week-end.' She yawned. 'And yet I shall hate to say goodbye to everyone here. It's been a happy time.'

'Yes,' Rosalind assented sleepily, 'but we can't stay here for ever—not that I want to, really. 'Night, Paula.'

Paula lay awake for a long time, staring into the darkness. She had thrust Bob Shaw to the back of her mind and was determined to keep him there till he was banished for ever. She knew that already he was receding into the past. Her thoughts winged themselves to the other side of the world, and she wondered dreamily what life had in store for herself and Rosalind out there if they actually went. New scenes, new friends—new loves, perhaps? Not for me, Paula decided, then amended it to—not for a long time anyway—and drifted off to sleep.

CHAPTER TWO

THE next morning the two girls went along to Tasmania House. Paula's "nice girl" was expecting them, and she took them into a smaller room at the back to await the interviews.

'Oh dear, I've got butterflies,' Rosalind whispered as she sat down on the edge of her chair. 'What if—' She broke off as the door opened and the girl appeared, followed by a tall, grey-haired woman with a pleasant, smiling face. Both girls stood up, and Matron nodded to them as she took her place behind a desk.

'Good morning. Do sit down.' She smoothed some papers in front of her and Paula saw that they were the application forms. Her knees felt quite weak as she and Rosalind resumed their seats. The door closed behind the receptionist and there was a short silence.

'Well now,' said Matron at last, and looking at the girls over her glasses, 'which is Miss Bruce, and which Miss Lane? Ah, yes.' She looked at Paula. 'So you want to nurse in Tasmania. Why?' She took off her glasses and polished them.

'I want to get as much varied experience in nursing as possible,' Paula replied, her voice slightly breathless. 'And—and I want to travel and see the world,' she finished.

'I see.' Matron turned to Rosalind and looked at the rosy face with its blue eyes and tip-tilted nose. 'And you?' she asked smilingly.

'Oh, I feel the same, Matron,' Rosalind said eagerly. 'We—we've talked about this for years, ever since we started our training, and—' She hesitated.

'Well now,' Matron interrupted, 'you've read the conditions of service, of course?' They murmured agreement, and Matron went on, 'You must be prepared to go anywhere, and at short notice. The bulk of the Tourist work is Maternity, and I see you both have your double certificates. The tour of duty is two years, and after that—' she paused and replaced her glasses, 'it rests with you—and the Department of Health. But we do need nurses, of the right sort.'

'Oh, we are the right sort,' Rosalind said earnestly, and Miss Norris laughed.

'Well now,' she said briskly, shuffling the papers together and standing up, 'we must fix up your medical, and chest X-ray, and—'

'Does that mean we're accepted, Matron?' Paula asked, eyes bright with anticipation.

'Yes. You'll need two references to take with you, of course.' She stood up and came from behind the desk. 'Well, my dears, the very best of luck,' she said, smiling and holding out a hand to each in turn. 'I shall look forward to seeing you in Hobart. Goodbye—for the present.'

'All right?' asked the girl in the outer room as, having waited for Miss Norris to leave, Paula and Rosalind now came out.

'Yes, it's in the bag,' Rosalind said, and gave Paula an excited hug round the waist.

'You'll love Tassie. By the way, my name's Ann Freeman. My family live just outside Hobart—a little place called Taroona. I'll give you a letter to them, if you like. My brother—' she broke off and hurried forward as a couple came wandering in.

'That's nice of her, isn't it?' Paula remarked to Rosalind. 'If everyone out there's as friendly—Come on, let's go.' She saw that Ann Freeman was likely to be busy for some time, and whispered to her as they passed, 'Thanks. We'll be in again to see you.'

The next few days were passed in a state of feverish activity. Medicals, X-ray, passports, testimonials, all were attended to. And on Saturday, having paid a last flying visit to Tasmania House to see Ann Freeman and get her letter of introduction, the two journeyed down into Somerset.

Rosalind was right about her mother. She looked at the two bright-eyed girls with envious eyes. 'How I'd love to come with you,' she said.

'Hey, what's all this?' broke in her husband, looking hurt.

'Don't worry, dear,' was the placid reply. 'You know I could never bring myself to desert my piglets, lambs and chicks—not to mention my old man. What I really mean is that I'd like to be young and adventurous again with the whole wide world beckoning.'

'Well, my dear, *I'm* beckoning you right now. For the last five minutes I've been waiting patiently for my supper. Rosy, *beckon* your mother to the table.'

Mrs Lane looked at her adopted daughter's lovely animated face. Thank goodness, she's getting over it already, she thought, her worries about Paula's affairs beginning to subside. What it is to be young and resilient. She smiled at the girl, and Paula gave her a quick, affectionate hug. 'Wish you were coming with us, Auntie,' she said.

After that, events moved quickly, and within a month of their interviews, the two girls were walking up the gangway of a noisy, crowded emigrant ship, bound for Australia. Neither of them had been on a large steamer before; and as the strip of dark brown water between the cliff-like side of the ship and Southampton Docks widened, they were almost speechless with excitement—and something else. For as they waved to the parents till they could see them no more, they both avoided each other's tell-tale eyes.

'It—won't be really long before we see them again,' Paula said jerkily. 'Two years will soon pass.' She turned with her back to the rail.

'Wish they could have come with us,' Rosalind muttered; and at the absurdity of the remark, they both started to laugh, and then felt very much better. And as they turned to go below, Paula realised that she had not thought of Bob for days. Already the pain had almost gone, and the feeling of emptiness had passed. So much had happened during the last month to help her in this dreary business of forgetting, and it was succeeding. Paula knew in her heart that if Bob had not actually married the other girl before breaking the news to her, she would have found it very much harder to accept it. There would have been the lingering hope that he would return to her. And yet, she thought, it could never have been the same. Confidence would have gone, and love without complete trust was a poor thing upon which to pin one's happiness.

So, as day followed day, Paula resolutely kept her thoughts fixed upon the new life ahead of her. And to her surprise she found that in quite a short time very little effort was needed. The daily life on board helped considerably. The girls found that it was almost impossible to be alone. Besides themselves, there were four others who shared the cabin with them, and as they remarked several times to each other, there was never a dull moment on this ship. Also, in crossing the Bay, they ran into rough weather, and as the stewardesses were run off their feet, the two girls willingly gave a hand.

But once they had passed Gibraltar and were well into the Mediterranean the weather cleared, the sun shone, the sea was like a sheet of blue glass, and everyone relaxed and began to enjoy themselves. Life on board settled down into a pleasant steady routine, and after a while one day seemed exactly like the next.

There were very few stops *en route*. In fact the first port in which the ship stopped long enough to enable passengers to go ashore was Colombo. There the two girls spent an enchanted afternoon in the native shops, fingering the exquisite wood and tortoiseshell ornaments and curios, and buying a few pieces of lovely hand-made lace. They had tea at the attractive Galle Face Hotel, situated at the end of the Esplanade, and overlooking the sea. In the evening they and a group of other passengers took taxis to the well-known Mount Lavinia, and had cool drinks at the beautiful rock-bound swimming club before driving back in the cool of the evening through banana and coconut groves.

'What a wonderful day!' Rosalind said with a sigh of enjoyment as the two climbed the gangplank to the ship's deck again. 'I shall be sorry when this voyage ends.'

'Um,' Paula agreed, 'but it will be nice to start our jobs again.'

'Keen type,' Rosalind observed. 'I can wait for it.'

One golden afternoon just a few days before their long journey was to come to an end, the two girls were sitting side by side on deck, one knitting, the other reading.

'I must try and get this finished before we disembark,' Rosalind murmured, holding up the half-finished sleeve of a cardigan. 'It's for Daddy's birthday.' She glanced sideways and saw that Paula's book had fallen to her lap, and she was staring silently out to sea. Rosalind watched her for a moment, then said, 'Penny for them.'

'I was thinking of Bob,' Paula said, after a pause.

'Oh!' Rosalind began, but Paula cut her short.

'I don't mean that I'm still—' she stopped, and a puzzled look came into her clear hazel eyes as she turned and looked at Rosalind. 'D'you know, Ross,' she began again haltingly, 'I've been thinking about it quite a lot lately, and I've wondered if I really and truly loved Bob. Oh, I know I was "in love," I just couldn't think of anything else; he had that effect on me. But—well, you see, it's all gone; so completely, almost as if it never happened.'

'I'm jolly glad to hear it,' Rosalind said, but Paula went on as if she had not heard.

'But it's rather frightening, Ross. You see, it could happen again, I suppose. And how *is* one to know love from infatuation?'

'By giving yourself time, of course. You didn't give yourself time to get to know Bob before you were engaged. You'll know better next time.'

A dimple appeared in Paula's smooth cheek. 'You're such a nice, down-to-earth person, Ross,' she said, and returned to her book.

At Melbourne, the girls found that they had to tran-ship before continuing their journey to Tasmania. They had expected to land in Hobart, but were told by the Melbourne port authorities that the migrant ships disembarked at Beauty Point at the entrance to the River Tamar.

'Oh, look, Ross,' Paula said, pointing. The little ship had just rounded a bluff and was entering the river. 'That must be Beauty Point; and it's certainly well named. D'you think that's apple-blossom?' She handed the binoculars to Rosalind and stood gazing, her elbows resting on the rail. 'Doesn't everything look green and fresh? I'd forgotten for the moment that it's springtime in Tasmania.' The two girls stood for a moment in silence their eyes flicking rapidly from one object on shore to another. It did not seem to be a big port, but it was literally a "point of beauty." The buildings were half screened by tall trees, and green fields came right down to the water's edge. The blossom which had caught Paula's eye earlier on was everywhere.

'I believe it is apple-blossom,' Paula said. 'It's the right time of year for it here, you know. The coast looks very—English, doesn't it, Ross?'

'Yes. Ann Freeman, the girl at Tasmania House, you know, said that it would remind us of home. Cornwall, she said. Remember? Paula, I feel *so* excited.' She lowered the glasses and looked at her companion with wide shining eyes. 'Just think. Very soon now we shall be setting foot in a new country—starting a new life. I wonder what will have happened to us in a year from now.'

Paula looked thoughtful. 'Well, it's up to us, I suppose,' she said at last. 'Anyway, whatever lies ahead, I'm *glad* I came.'

'And I,' Rosalind agreed. Then, linking arms, the two went below to finish their packing. And everyone else seemed to have the same idea, Paula thought, as she edged her way into the crowded cabin. Halfway through the job, someone who had just come in called out, 'Oh, there you are, Miss Bruce. You're being called on the loudspeaker.'

'Me!' Paula exclaimed in surprise, and looked at Rosalind.

'Come on,' said the latter at once. 'Someone from the hospital, perhaps.' The two hurried out and found that the ship had already docked. Halfway up the steps towards the deck Paula heard the summons. 'Will Miss Paula Bruce please come to the saloon where Mr Deane from the Department of Health, Hobart, is waiting to see her.'

'Mr Deane!' Rosalind whispered excitedly. 'I wonder who he is?'

Paula made no reply, for by this time they had reached the entrance to the saloon. It was crowded—passengers, visitors, port and customs authorities, ship's staff, all sitting and standing about. Paula looked about her helplessly. Now which, among all these strangers, she wondered, was Mr Deane? 'Well, I don't know—' she was beginning to say, when a pleasantly deep voice right at her elbow said,

'Good morning. Miss Paula Bruce?'

She turned, and her eyes travelled up—and up. He was tall and thin and his clothes hung loosely upon him. His face was brown and craggy and his grey eyes looked unsmilingly into hers.

'Yes,' Paula said, her ready smile flashing out, 'and this,' she turned her head, 'is Rosalind Lane.' The tall man bowed, and smiled rather stiffly.

'Welcome to Tasmania,' he said, and held out a hand to each in turn. 'I hope you will be very happy here.' He put a hand into his breast pocket. 'My card,' he said, handing it to Paula. She glanced up at him as she took it, and for a brief moment their eyes met and held. Then he smiled quite charmingly, showing white irregular teeth, and said, 'I'll wait for you here. Are you ready to go ashore? I'm taking you both along to Hobart in my car. It's a two hours' run.' Paula returned his smile and blushed for no apparent reason.

'Thank you,' she said. 'We'll be as quick as possible,' and hurried to overtake Rosalind who had gone on ahead.

'He's rather nice,' Rosalind observed in a low tone as they hurried below to collect hand luggage. 'What's on the card, Paula?'

' "Christopher Deane, F.R.C.S.",' Paula read out, then added, ' "Department of Health, Hobart, Tasmania." ' The two looked at each other.

'Well,' Rosalind said, 'I certainly didn't expect to be met on board by the surgeon, did you?'

'We must be V.I.P.s,' Paula assured her, the corners of her mouth turning up. She took a compact from her bag and dabbed at her nose. 'Come on, hurry, we mustn't keep Christopher waiting.'

'I wonder if he's married,' Rosalind murmured a few minutes later as she hurriedly crammed last-minute things into an already bulging handbag.

'Sure to be; he's much too nice not to have been caught in the "tender trap" years ago. You ready?' But in spite of her casual dismissal of Rosalind's comment, Paula herself had been wondering the same thing. 'Come on, Ross, Mr Deane is taking us to Hobart in his car. About two hours, he said it takes, so we must hurry.'

Half an hour later, with customs cleared and all the formalities completed, Christopher Deane led the two girls to a large, comfortable-looking car. He stowed the cases in the boot, then opened the car doors.

'Ready?' he said, looking at Paula. 'There's room for one in front, if you'd—' he paused. 'Perhaps you would sit here beside me, Miss Bruce; and then, later on, change places with Miss—er—Lane.

As the car started off, Paula looked about her with bright eyes and parted lips. Here she was at last, starting a new life, in a new country. And yet it did not look so very different from home, she thought, as the car moved

up the main street. But once away from the streets and
buildings she caught her breath in amazed delight. For
all about them spread the apple orchards. To right and to
left, as far as the eye could see, and looking like huge
pink and white bouquets, the squat trees were almost
hidden under their crown of blossom. 'So it *was* apple-
blossom we could see,' she said, turning to look at Rosalind. Christopher Deane looked at her pink cheeks and
shining hazel eyes.

'Tasmania is known as the Apple Island,' he said,
'You've come just at the right time. Beautiful, isn't it?'

'It's like fairyland,' Paula replied softly. She was
noticing more differences as the car sped along. The
houses and cottages they passed were built mostly of
wood, and were long and low in shape. They were
washed in gay, bright colours.

'Weatherboard,' Mr Deane said in reply to her question. At that moment the car rounded a bend and both
girls exclaimed in delight.

'Paula, look at that marvellous bank of mimosa,'
Rosalind said, leaning forward and pointing.

'We call it wattle out here,' Christopher Deane
remarked. 'You'll see plenty of that. It grows almost
everywhere.'

'There's a charming house,' Paula said, looking to her
left. It was long and low and painted white. A porticoed
verandah ran the entire length with a large dignified
entrance in the centre. At both ends were clumps of tall
rangy-looking trees with bluish-green foliage, and in
front of the house was a wide drive between smooth
green lawns.

'Yes, that's real Colonial style,' he told her. 'It was
probably built by convicts many years ago.'

'What are the tall trees called?' Rosalind asked.

'They're gums; also very common in Tasmania, and
on the mainland. There are many different kinds. Those
over there are red gums.' There was silence for a short
time, then Christopher Deane glanced sideways at his
companion and said,

'What made you come out here?'

'I wanted to start seeing the world I live in.' Paula turned and smiled at him as she spoke. His white teeth showed in an answering smile.

'That's a very good reason,' he said. 'And I hope you won't be disappointed in any of it.'

Hobart was reached just before midday, and Mr Deane took the girls at once to the Department of Health in Davey Street. It was a large square red-brick building. 'I'll take you along to Miss Needham's office,' he said to Paula. 'She is the Inspecting Sister. She'll fix you up at the Nurses' Club, and tell you when you will be starting your jobs. Soon, I imagine.' He smiled down at her as he spoke. 'They're short-handed, I believe, at present.' He stopped speaking, then after a slight pause, added, 'Would you—and Miss Lane—care to have dinner with me tonight? I'd like to show you Wrest Point. It's worth a visit, and you may not be in Hobart for long.' Paula's heart gave a little jump of excitement. This is going to be fun, she thought.

'Thank you,' she said. 'It's very kind of you. I'd like to very much—' She looked questioningly at Rosalind, who nodded vigorously.

The interview with Miss Needham did not take long. She was a brisk middle-aged woman sitting behind a desk piled high with papers.

'Glad to see you,' she greeted the girls. 'We can certainly use you. I hope you're eager for work because I'm packing you off tomorrow to Dover. It's on the south coast. Small hospital, visiting doctor. You'll like it; good place to start from.' She rattled on for a few more minutes, then called her assistant and told her to take the new arrivals to the Nurses' Club in McQuarrie Street.

'Well, we breathe again,' Paula said about ten minutes later, looking round the bright cheerful little bedroom at the club. 'I suppose it's all right, but there were heaps of questions I wanted to ask her.'

'You can put them tomorrow,' Rosalind said comfortably. 'The girl who brought us here said we wouldn't be leaving till nine or ten. Bags of time. I wonder what Dover's like. Paula, aren't you thrilled about tonight? Christopher's a pet, isn't he? I think he's fallen for you.'

'Don't be an idiot,' Paula laughed, but with sudden colour showing in her cheeks. 'He's married; sure to be. He's just being kind to two strangers.'

'Well, I hope he doesn't bring his wife with him,' Rosalind said gaily, and began to unpack.

Christopher did not bring a wife with him. Instead, he arrived at the Nurses' Club with a man companion—a Dr Sinclair, a merry-looking young man about ten years younger than himself. Rosalind's eyes lit up when she saw the two get out of the car.

'A foursome,' she whispered to Paula. 'Goody!'

Paula again sat in the front of the car beside Christopher Deane. 'We'll have a drive round before going to Wrest Point,' he said. 'How did you get on at the interview?'

Paula laughed. 'All right, I think,' she said. 'We didn't get a word in edgeways, but I did gather that we're off to a place called Dover tomorrow.'

'Tomorrow, eh?'

She glanced quickly at him and thought he sounded disappointed; then, as he said nothing more, she decided, regretfully, that she had been mistaken. Christopher Deane puzzled and attracted Paula at the same time. Against the cool, guarded look in the grey eyes was his rare, charming smile. She wondered what age he was. About thirty-seven or eight, she thought, and had to admit to herself that she liked him—very much. But her recent experience with Bob Shaw had made Paula cautious, and now she turned away, dismissing Christopher Deane from her mind.

Rosalind and this Dr Sinclair seem to be hitting it off, Paula thought, hearing voices and laughter from the back seat. She saw that the car was now turning in at the gates of Wrest Point Hotel, and presently they stopped before the entrance. 'Here we are,' Christopher said, opening the door on Paula's side. 'There are the cloak-rooms, along to the left.'

'Gosh, Paula, isn't this marvellous?' Rosalind murmured a few minutes later as, side by side, the two girls entered the dining room. Christopher and his companion came forward to meet them, and the waiter led them all to a table at the far side. A huge window overlooked Sandy Bay. Dr Sinclair waved an arm.

'What do you think of the view?' he asked with possessive pride. The two girls looked out on to the wide sweep of water. Lights were just beginning to twinkle. Boats with taut, gaily-coloured sails skimmed the surface and disappeared behind other and bigger ones. Just below the window Paula could see gardens and lawns, and beyond that a narrow path which followed the line of the coast. She drew a deep breath and sighed.

'It's perfectly lovely,' she said softly, and was rather excitedly conscious of Christopher Deane's eyes on her face. She smiled at him and he moved a step nearer. 'I'm so glad you asked us,' Paula added.

'There are many beauty spots round here,' he said, paused, then added in a rather abrupt voice, 'I would—like to show you some, if I may. Dover is not very far off.' Paula felt her cheeks redden as she met the brief glance of his eyes. She felt ridiculously happy all at once.

The waiter was still hovering near as they turned from the window and took their seats; and at that moment a party of men, rather a noisy party, appeared at the door. Paula looked over her shoulder as a particularly loud laugh came across to them. She looked—then seemed to freeze in her chair. Her lips parted dryly, and her wide eyes became fixed in a fascinated stare. For the moment Paula was oblivious of her companions. She was conscious of only one person. The man at the other table. The man who, a short two months before, had meant the whole world to her—Bob Shaw.

CHAPTER THREE

WITH an effort that was physically painful, Paula dragged her eyes away from that well-remembered face. Bob had not seen her, but she was afraid it was only a matter of time. Her thoughts scurried back and forth in a dazed kind of way. What was he doing here? Of course, his ship! But Paula had got the impression that he was giving up his job and settling in Mexico. Perhaps he couldn't right away. In any case, and this was a more cheering thought, tankers never stayed long in port—a day at the most, Bob had once told her. Paula took a swift side glance at Christopher Deane and saw that he was talking to Rosalind; and as she watched his whimsical smile and air of quiet self-assurance, Paula knew that the spell Bob Shaw had put upon her was gone for ever. The knowledge that he was there, just a few yards from her, meant just nothing at all. Emotionally, it was as if he had never been. To Paula it was a sobering thought, and she hoped intensely that he would go without having seen her.

'You're looking very thoughtful.' It was Christopher Deane speaking, and as Paula did not at once reply, he added, 'I hope you like scallops. They're a speciality here. Miss Lane assures me that *she* does.'

'I don't think I've ever had them.' Paula had almost recovered her composure and was determined to keep her back firmly turned upon that table near the door. She was out to enjoy herself, and was not going to let Bob Shaw spoil it for her. She smiled at Christopher Deane. 'But I'd love to try them, Mr Deane.'

'Need we be so formal?' Dr Sinclair broke in, smiling round the circle. 'I'm Jack, and our learned friend here,' he bowed in Christopher's direction, 'is known to his confederates as Chris.' He turned to Rosalind and waited.

28

'Well!' she said, and laughed. 'Mr Deane—er—Chris knows *our* names, but I'm Rosalind, and this is Paula.'

The waiter with the soup arrived at that moment, and for a time there was silence. Then Paula caught Christopher's eye and he smiled at her and said, 'Jack makes me sound horribly elderly, don't you think, Paula?' Though he spoke lightly she saw that he was waiting for her to reply.

'Oh, I don't think so,' Paula said, smiling back at him. The meal progressed smoothly, the scallops being a great success, and by the time it had reached the coffee and liqueur stage, all four were talking as easily as if they had known each other for months instead of one day. Presently the band struck up some dance music and several couples made their way into the centre of the room.

'Like to dance, Rosalind?' It was Jack Sinclair speaking.

'Love to,' she replied, setting down her coffee cup and following him on to the dance space.

I'm afraid I'm not much of a performer,' Christopher said, looking at Paula, 'but if you'd—'

'I'd rather sit and talk,' Paula replied promptly. She was fairly safe, she felt, sitting there with her back turned squarely to that other table. But then another thought struck her. Would Bob notice Rosalind? If he did he would almost certainly recognise her, as they had met on various occasions. Paula looked out of the window to the scene of dream-like beauty below and hoped fervently that Bob and his friends had gone. She dared not look round to make sure, and was suddenly conscious that Christopher was watching her with a slightly puzzled frown. Paula smiled brightly at him, and he leaned across the table, his level grey eyes looking straight into hers. Paula's heart gave a quick, uneven beat.

'I'm sorry you're leaving Hobart so soon, Paula,' he said.

'So am I.' She looked down at her clasped hands.

'Very sorry, but—' hazel eyes met grey, 'I'm awfully glad to have had this one lovely evening, anyway.' Christopher waited a second, then said,

'But you'll be coming to Hobart for your days off, everyone does; and I shall hope to see you then. In any case,' his voice dropped a note, 'I'll be along tomorrow morning to see you off to Dover if you—' His voice died away as another and louder voice sounded just above his head.

'Why, look who's here!' Paula jerked her head up and stared into the flushed, smiling face of Bob Shaw—her ex-fiancé. Her heart began to beat with heavy, uneven thuds. 'I've just seen your pal and she told me you'd just arrived.' There was amazement—and something else—in his voice as he watched Paula's face. Then he glanced briefly at the politely surprised face of Christopher Deane, and laughed again. 'My, but I'm glad to see you, Paula. I wondered why I hadn't heard. I wrote several times. Didn't you—'

'Oh, hello, Bob,' Paula broke in feverishly. What did he mean by saying he'd written several times? She'd had nothing after that horrible callous letter telling her of his marriage. Why should he write again after that? Paula saw that Christopher was watching her. 'I—this is Bob Shaw,' she gabbled nervously. 'We—er—we knew each other in England, and—' She was about to introduce Christopher when Bob broke into another loud laugh. He put a familiar hand on Paula's shoulder, and said, with a meaning look,

'Knew each other in England! Paula, my sweet, isn't that drawing it rather mild? I'll say we certainly *did* know each other.' Paula's cheeks were suddenly crimson. She moved sharply, and gave a swift glance at Christopher. What must he be thinking? But she saw that he was watching the other man with a cool stare.

'This is Mr Deane,' Paula said abruptly. She was furious with this man with whom she had once been so madly in love. Why did he not go? Surely he could see that he was unwelcome, and rightly so.

'Well, well, we must certainly have a talk, exchange news and all that. I've got lots to tell you, Paula. Come and dance. D'you mind?' casually to the other man. Paula swallowed, but before she could think of a reply, Christopher replied courteously,

'Not at all. It rests with Miss Bruce. I'm sure she will want to exchange news with her—friend.' Was there a slight hesitation before the last two words? He stood up, and Paula, after a second's indecision, rose also. The situation had got beyond her control. She did not want to dance with Bob—in fact, she wanted to have nothing more to do with him. But she couldn't very well say so here. She had a strong suspicion that he had been drinking, and might make a scene if she refused. Perhaps it would be better to go with him, have it out, and return as soon as possible. Stiffly Paula turned and followed Bob to the dance floor. She glanced briefly at him as they joined the other dancers, and it was as if she were looking into the face of a stranger. Yet this was the man who, a short two months before, had meant all the world to her. 'Well—' she began, but he interrupted her.

'Paula,' his voice came low and urgent, but Paula was not listening. She was recalling his ill-chosen words, and their possible effect on the other man. She had taken an instant liking to Christopher Deane and felt sure that it was the same with him. Now it looked as if everything might well be spoilt almost before it had begun; and by the very man who had jilted her so short a time ago. Paula turned on him now with angry eyes, but his voice came again. 'I had to see you, Paula. I *must* talk to you. I—'

'There's no need to talk—or apologise, if that's what you're going to do. In fact, you've talked a little too much already.' Paula's voice shook, but she was determined to end this situation as soon as possible. His face reddened as he looked at her.

'I wasn't going to apologise,' he muttered. 'Too late for that. I know I don't deserve your forgiveness, but there *is* something I want you to know. I'm hoping that you'll understand and—forgive.'

'Well, what is it?' Paula asked through set teeth. 'I'm listening.'

Bob looked at her with reproach. 'Paula, that's not like you, but—' he hesitated for a moment, then said softly, 'Darling, I'm not married after all.'

She stared at him, then dragged her eyes away, a horrid feeling of dismay at her heart. His words meant nothing to her now, but what of him? What did he expect her reaction to be? There was silence between them. Paula knew he was waiting for her to speak; then his voice came again, low in her ear.

'Paula dear, it was all a mistake.' His arms tightened round her. 'Darling, it was you I loved all the time,' he whispered. 'Thank God I found out before it was too late. I wrote to tell you, but had no reply. I couldn't understand it, but of course you were on your way—you didn't receive it?' She shook her head, hardly hearing his words. Frantic thoughts were twisting and turning in her mind. This is awful, she thought, but it's all his fault, and it's all too late. A wave of anger almost choked her. What right had he to think that he could drop her, then pick her up again when he wanted? She looked at him with narrowed eyes.

'You needn't say any more.' Her voice trembled slightly. 'I'm not blaming you, but as far as I'm concerned, everything's finished. We're all washed up, you and I.'

He stared at her in silence, his mouth slowly opening. 'Paula, you can't mean that,' he muttered, then drew a long breath. 'You can't have changed—so soon. Why, you always said—'

'I know what I said. And I did then, but it's all over, I tell you. Please take me back—'

'I don't believe you,' he interrupted roughly. 'Look, Paula, we can't talk like this.' He glanced swiftly round and attempted to draw her towards an empty table for two. 'Come over here.'

'No!' she said sharply. 'I'm with a party and I'm going back.'

'Look,' Bob said, his lips set in a thin line, 'if you don't come and listen to what I have to say, I'll come with you and join your party, and let them hear, too.' Paula stared at him for a tense moment, uncertain whether to believe him or not, but there was an obstinate set to his chin.

'Very well,' she said, her eyes glinting with anger. 'But it will make no difference.'

'What will you have to drink?' he asked as they reached the table and he pulled out a chair for Paula.

'Nothing, thank you,' she replied, 'and please say what you have to say as quickly as possible.' She glanced swiftly in the direction of the other table and saw that Christopher had lighted a cigarette, and was smoking and looking out of the window. Paula tapped a foot impatiently. The dance was still going on, and if she could get away quickly from Bob this little interlude might not be noticed. He leant forward and put a hand over hers. Paula snatched it away.

'I don't know why we're sitting here,' she said angrily. 'Please say whatever it is you want to say, and allow me to go back to my friends.' Bob looked at her in silence, then slowly shook his head.

'I just can't believe it's you talking, Paula,' he said, then leant forward and added in a low voice, 'It was all a mistake—the other girl, I mean. I've got no excuse, I know, but it seemed such a long time since I'd seen you, darling, and—I just drifted into it. Oh, Paula,' he tried again to take her hand, but she kept it in her lap, 'why didn't you marry me when I asked you? This would never have happened then.'

'We went over all that long ago, Bob,' she said in a more gentle voice, 'and there's no point in going over it again. I'm sorry—about everything, but it's too late as far as I'm concerned. What happened was a shock to me, but it's all over. Please believe that.'

'Paula,' his voice became more urgent, 'is it really too late?' He looked at her imploringly and her heart softened. But slowly she shook her head.

'I'm sorry, Bob,' she said again, 'but I'm afraid it is, and that's all there is to it. People change, and perhaps I never really loved you.'

'Oh yes, you did, and I believe you still do; but you're angry, and I don't blame—'

'It's no use, I tell you,' Paula interrupted. She saw the expression in his eyes change.

'I suppose it's that snooty-looking chap over there,' he said, a nasty twist to his mouth. 'Who is he, anyway?'

'It doesn't matter who he is; and anyway he has nothing to do with it. I only met him today,' Paula replied. 'Please be sensible, Bob. You brought this on yourself, you know.' She hesitated, then said, 'I must get back now. Goodbye. No, please,' as he rose to his feet. 'There's no need for you to come with me. Good luck, Bob,' and turning quickly, she vanished in the direction of the ladies' room. She heard him say something about writing as she went, but took no notice.

Paula looked at her flushed face in the mirror, and tried to still the trembling of her lips. Though she had hidden it till now, the meeting with Bob, and his news, had been a shock to her. As he had talked, Paula had remembered, with a sick kind of regret, all that he had meant to her. She had felt contempt not only for him, but for herself, for the swift change in her feelings. Tears welled into her eyes, and overflowed. Why did this have to happen now? she thought. My very first day in a new country. She'd been happy and confident, but now she was confused and muddled, and felt somehow cheap. Hastily she took out a handkerchief, and dabbed at her eyes, then swiftly got to work with powder and lipstick.

At the door Paula waited for the music to stop, then gave a quick glance round the room. The table where she had sat with Bob was unoccupied and there was no sign of him anywhere. She drew a quick breath of relief.

Rosalind gave Paula a side-glance as she rejoined the party, but said nothing. There was an expression on her face that Paula did not like. She had noticed with intense disappointment as she approached the table that Christopher was not there. Jack Sinclair stood up and pulled a chair out for her. His face was unsmiling.

'Chris had to go, I'm afraid,' he said. 'A call from the hospital, I think. He asked me to make his apologies.'

'Oh, I am sorry,' Paula said, a horrible feeling of depression descending upon her, 'but perhaps he'll be back?'

'Well, he didn't seem to think so.' He did not look at her as he spoke. Paula's face flushed uncomfortably.

'What a pity!' she said. 'It's spoilt his evening, hasn't it?' She was miserably conscious that it was she who had spoilt his evening, and everyone else's, too. Paula glanced at Rosalind's unresponsive face, and there was an uneasy silence at the table. She was glad when, soon after this, the party broke up and Jack took them both back to the Nurses' Club.

Rosalind hardly waited till they were in their bedroom before turning upon Paula. 'What got into you?' she demanded. 'It was bad luck enough running into Bob Shaw, but did you *have* to dance with him, and then go and sit *tête-à-tête* holding hands? What a nerve that man has, and I'm surprised at you, Paula. I suppose it's started all over again. Well, don't forget—'

'Ross, you've got it all wrong,' Paula interrupted. 'I had to—dance with him. But nothing's started again; and as for holding hands—listen, Ross,' and Paula told her everything that had happened, from the time when Bob had come up to her till she had returned to the table to find Christopher gone. When she repeated the words which Bob had used at the table with Christopher there, Rosalind stared at her in dismay.

'It was awful, Ross,' Paula said, sitting down suddenly on the side of her bed. 'It sounded so—cheap and familiar. Almost as if—' she stopped, an expression of distaste on her face. 'D'you see now why I had to get him away? He kept saying he had lots to tell me. I think he'd been drinking.'

'Lots to tell you!' Rosalind exclaimed angrily. 'I bet he

had at that. Did he remember, by the way, that he's married now?'

'He's not.' Paula's voice was flat and expressionless. She looked across at Rosalind and saw the look of anger on her face change to one of bewilderment.

'Not married!' she said, and paused, staring at Paula's face. 'But, Paula, he wrote and told you he *was* married. I don't get this.'

'I know,' Paula said, nodding her head slowly, 'I've been thinking about that. He wrote and told me about the other girl, and said—these were the exact words— "By the time you get this letter I shall be married." '

Rosalind looked at her in silence, then sat down on the side of the other bed. 'I see,' she said at last. 'So he changed his mind at the last moment—or perhaps the girl did. Well, why didn't he let you know? Though I'm jolly glad he didn't.'

'He says he wrote several times,' Paula said wearily.

'Do you believe that?' Paula shrugged her shoulders, got up and went to the dressing table.

'I suppose so,' she said. 'We did leave London almost at once; but I should have thought any letters would have been forwarded. In any case, Ross, it makes no difference to me now, and I told him so.'

Rosalind looked relieved. 'I'm glad of that, Paula,' she said. 'He was never the right one for you. But what did he say?'

'Oh, what does it matter?' Paula turned abruptly away. 'I'm sick of the whole business.' There was silence as both girls started to undress. 'I suppose—Chris saw me sitting there with him? Oh, damn! Sorry to have spoilt the party, Ross.'

'Don't worry about that,' Rosalind replied. 'Pity about Christopher, though. D'you think he noticed Bob's words? I do hope not, because I think our Mr Deane rather likes you.'

Paula picked up a brush and started to brush her hair. 'I like him,' she remarked, and picked up the comb. 'However, it can't be helped now, I suppose. Oh!' she made an exasperated movement. 'Apart from anything else, I'd hate him—or anyone, for that matter—to think that—' she stopped, and Rosalind could hear her quick, agitated breathing.

'Yes, I know,' she said slowly. She tried to see Paula's face as she added casually, 'Jack Sinclair told me that Christopher's not married—at least, not now. He's a widower, with a small daughter. They live just outside Hobart, at a place called Lenah Valley.'

Paula turned and looked at her, the brush poised in one hand. 'No,' she said, and smiled suddenly at Rosalind. 'Somehow, I didn't think he was.'

'What will you do, Paula?' Rosalind looked at her curiously before climbing into bed.

'I don't quite know, but I *must* try to think of a way to clear up any misunderstandings.' She turned and looked at Rosalind with bright eyes.

'Yes, but how?' said the latter. 'Will you write? We leave tomorrow morning, you know.'

Paula looked thoughtful. 'Yes, I know,' she said quietly. 'Now I wonder—Christopher did say that he would come to see us off, but—' she looked at Rosalind and the latter slowly shook her head.

'Somehow I don't think so, Paula,' she said regretfully. 'You see, just after Chris had asked Jack to make his apologies to you, he turned to me and said goodbye. He shook hands and said that he was afraid he wouldn't be seeing either of us for some time as he was shortly leaving for the mainland. I don't know if he meant for good or not. I didn't like to question Jack. But it all sounded very definite.'

'Oh!' Paula stared at her. Her face was pale and she suddenly looked tired and depressed. 'Looks as if he did think things, doesn't it? Well, I can't blame him. It did sound pretty awful, and he doesn't really know me—us.' She turned away and got into bed. 'Not a very good beginning to my first day in Tasmania.' She sighed, then grinned at Rosalind over the sheet. 'Never mind: I'll think of something.'

Rosalind looked at her, hesitated, then said, 'How did you feel about—Bob?'

Slow colour crept up into Paula's cheeks.

'I wonder now if I ever really knew him,' she said abruptly. 'It was like being with a stranger; and not a very nice stranger, either. It's made me see myself a little more clearly too; and that's not a particularly nice picture, either.'

'I don't see that you have anything to blame yourself for,' Rosalind remarked loyally.

Paula sighed. 'Well, let's forget it, anyway,' she said. 'You ready for bed?' And as the light clicked off, 'I want never to see Bob Shaw again!'

CHAPTER FOUR

PAULA was some time getting off to sleep that first night in Tasmania. The events of the evening had been upsetting enough, without the added disappointment of knowing that Christopher Deane had changed his mind about coming to see her off to Dover in the morning. She could understand his reaction to Bob Shaw's ill-chosen words, which had unfortunately been strengthened by her own action in dancing, and then sitting talking with him. Had it really appeared that they were holding hands? Paula wondered. What a muddle! Was there anything she could do about it? Regretfully she decided that at present there was nothing. It was hateful to have to leave it like this, Paula thought; but if, at any time in the future, she were to meet him again, she'd try to let him know the true facts. He might not be interested, but at least he would know she was not that sort of girl and that was what mattered most; and on that thought, Paula turned over in bed, and drifted off to sleep.

She awoke to bright sunshine which was partly blotted out by Rosalind's plump figure leaning half out of the window. She turned her head as Paula sat up. 'It's a gorgeous day,' she called. 'Come and look at the view.'

Paula looked at her watch instead, and saw that it was nearly eight. 'We've got to hurry,' she said. 'Breakfast is at eight, and the coach goes at nine. The view will have to wait. Have you washed yet?'

'No, but I won't be a minute,' and there was silence except for an occasional rustle and the quick breathing of the two girls as they washed, dressed and combed their hair into place.

And at exactly five to nine they arrived at the coach stop. The coach was being loaded up as they got there.

Rosalind was in front, and as Paula followed her, she took a quick glance all round. He might relent and come, she thought, but there was no sign of that tall figure and brown craggy face. So that's that—for the present, she mentally decided, and sat down beside Rosalind. The coach was being loaded with sacks, bales and boxes of all kinds. It was amazing what was being stowed away in the boot.

Miss Needham from the Department of Health suddenly appeared. She waved to the two girls, and climbed up into the coach to say goodbye.

'You'll enjoy the drive,' she said. 'It's through lovely country. The coach stops at Huonville, and again at Franklin, where you can get drinks and snacks. You'll be at Dover in time for midday dinner.' She looked out of the window. 'They're ready to start. I must go. Well, goodbye, my dears, and good luck. I'll be seeing you soon, I've no doubt. Everyone comes to Hobart for their days off.' That was what Christopher had said, Paula thought.

'Goodbye, Miss Needham,' they said, then turned with lively interest to the start of the coach journey. It was a golden morning, and Paula was in tune with it. No one could be depressed on a day like this, she thought, gazing wide-eyed out of the coach window. The town was soon left behind, and as they turned off the main road, and came to quiet wooded country, the girls had their first real view of Mount Wellington with its glittering white cap of snow soaring high into the blue, cloudless sky.

'Ross,' Paula said, gripping her companion's hand, 'the very first day off we have, we'll go up there, right to the very top. There's a road snaking its way up there. Can you see it?' She pointed.

'You're right,' said a middle-aged man who was sitting in the seat behind. 'The road does go to the top; and a wonderful view you get too. There's a look-out right at the summit and you can see almost the whole of the island.'

'It must be marvellous.' Paula turned to smile at him, and Rosalind said excitedly,

'Yes, we will. We'll take some food, hire a car, and spend the day there.'

'There's a hotel at the top,' put in their neighbour. 'You can get a good meal there. You just out from home?'

Paula assented, and for the rest of the journey he made it his business to point out all the places of interest. His wife, a plump, motherly-looking woman who sat beside him, joined in occasionally. For some time the road wound round and about, skirting the great mountain. Then it started to climb into the foothills. Towering pines, and the shorter, more compact firs lined each side of the road. The air, despite increasing coldness, had a delightfully aromatic tang.

'You're in for a treat now,' said their self-appointed guide as the coach approached a sharp bend, and as it curved round slowly in low gear both girls gave excited exclamations of wonder and delight.

'Gosh, Paula, look at that!' Rosalind said breathlessly. The two gazed with parted lips at the scene spread out before them. They were now at the highest point of their journey, and from then on the road wound its way down again. Before them stretched the steeply-descending ranks of pine trees. And beyond them, as the ground levelled out, were the squat, compact patches of the apple orchards in the distance. And further on still was a magnificent, uninterrupted view of Hòbart harbour. It stretched to right and left, a broad streak of brightest blue and dotted with liners, yachts, and bright-sailed boats of every description.

'Oh, beautiful!' Paula breathed, her wide hazel eyes taking it all in, and added, 'I'm *sorry* for people who are dead.'

Rosalind stared at her rapt face then started to laugh. 'What a thing to say!' she giggled, and there came a chuckle from behind.

'What I mean is,' Paula explained, 'the world is such a

wonderful place, so full of beauty and interest every-where, that however long one lived it could never be long enough. D'you see?'

'Yes, I think I know what you mean. Look,' Rosalind pointed, 'we're starting to go down now.'

'Yes, we'll be in apple country soon,' said their friendly neighbour. 'We stop for a short time at Huon-ville, that's on the river, then the coach goes over the bridge. You'll enjoy that, it's a bonzer river. After Franklin, our next stop is Dover. This country we're passing through now is berry country.' He waved an arm, and the two girls looked with interest at the stretches of low green bushes which came down almost to the side of the road. 'This is Longley we're going through now,' he added. 'The bushes you can see on either side are strawberries, raspberries, and berries of all kinds.'

The girls noticed that the houses were of the kind they had seen all along the route—long and low, and built of gaily-painted weatherboard. They were all flanked by row upon row of fresh green, dappled with the blossom of some of the berry trees.

Presently they came to the bridge which crossed the River Huon, and from then on their route lay along a path which followed the curves and bends of the river.

'Where are you making for, dears?' enquired the wife of the friendly man behind them. And when Paula told her, she exclaimed, 'Oh, you'll be the two new Sisters for the hospital. Sister Morton, who's there now, told us that you were coming out straight from home.'

'Have you been out here long?' Paula enquired, struck by the use of the word 'home' by both their neighbours. The wife laughed.

'Oh, we were born here,' she said. 'And our parents. I've never been to England, but everyone in Tassie refers to it as home. We are of English descent,' she added proudly.

It was almost midday when the road they were on suddenly branched away from the river and plunged once more into apple orchard country. And again they were surrounded by the delicate pink and white of the blossom. Then, quite excitingly, as the coach rounded a corner they were again in view of the sea.

'Not long now,' said the friendly woman behind, smiling at the two girls as they turned to her enquiringly. 'The hospital is right on the coast, just a couple of miles further on.' Soon the coach passed through the village of Dover, a little way inland, then out to the coast again, passing several shops, a few houses and a post office. Then along for another half-mile, and at last in through some wide gates and on to a circular drive. It stopped in front of a long, low red-brick buliding.

'Here we are,' said their friend at the back, and Paula looked and smiled.

'Doesn't it look small, after St Just's?' she said to Rosalind, 'but what a gorgeous position.' The driver came round and opened the door.

'I've got your cases out, girls,' he said in a friendly way. 'This is it.' They got up, said goodbye to the couple behind, and clambered down from the coach. As it rolled off, they stood for a moment, looking about them. On both sides of the big front door were beds of red and yellow tulips. Just outside the entrance gates was the main road, and beyond that the beach and sea.

'Gosh!' Rosalind said, her eyes bright with anticipation, 'I'm glad I brought plenty of swim and beach suits. Look, Paula, there's a jetty and a diving float. I'm going to like this place.'

Paula laughed, then turned as she heard a door behind them open. A girl stood framed in the front entrance. She was dark, with brown eyes, and was in spotless white uniform from top to bottom—head square, overall, stockings and shoes.

'Hello,' she said, smiling at the other two, and came forward with outstretched hand. 'Are you Sister Bruce?' as Paula stepped forward, 'and this is Sister Lane?' The three girls shook hands all round. 'My name's Nancy Morton. Come in, and I'll show you to your rooms.'

Paula and Rosalind followed her into a square hall from which several doors led off. 'Let me help you with your cases,' she said. 'I'm afraid we have only one domestic and she's busy with dinner just now. Come along this way,' and she opened a door and led the two girls along a short passage. 'Here are your rooms,' she said, stopping, 'next door to each other. I've moved my things out, so you can settle in straightaway. But first, dinner, of course. You must be famished. Come back to the hall when you're ready, and I'll take you to the dining room where you'll meet the rest of the staff—I hope.' She laughed. 'We're frightfully busy. Three maternity cases, one already in the labour ward, and the next due any minute now. Also a heart case who needs constant watching. D'you think, after lunch, you could—' She hesitated, and Paula said at once,

'Of course. We're ready to start any time, just as soon as we've unpacked our uniforms.'

'Good,' said the other girl, and went out, closing the door behind her.

'Well, well!' Rosalind said, plumping down on her knees before a suitcase. 'We're on the job, my girl.'

'The overalls are going to look a bit crumpled,' Paula said, struggling with the keys of her case, 'but it can't be helped. In any case, they'll probably be too busy to notice, and nylon soon shakes out. Good, here's mine,' and standing up, she began a rapid change.

Within ten minutes the two girls were back in the hall where they found Sister Morton waiting for them. 'I say,' she said, looking them up and down, 'all ready for work, eh? You have been quick. Doc Renwick will be very pleased to see you, so will Vera Watts. She's the other Sister who is leaving. We both go tomorrow. I've had instructions to hand over to Sister Bruce, but when we can fit it in I really don't know. However, we'll cross our bridges when we come to them. This way.'

She pulled aside a heavy curtain, and then they saw that the dining room was a partitioned-off part of the hall. Nancy Morton led the way to the table. A lean, sandy-haired man with a humorous face was sitting there. He stood up as Nancy introduced him as Dr Renwick, then immediately resumed his seat and went on with his meal.

'You must excuse me,' he said between mouthfuls, 'but I expect Sister has told you that we have plenty on our plates just at present. In fact, my wife is here giving a hand till you're ready to take over.' He smiled at the two girls in an absent-minded sort of way.

'We're ready now, as soon as we've finished lunch,' Paula said, starting on the plate of soup which had just been placed before her. 'We've been on holiday for over two months, so—'

'Ready for work, eh?' he said, putting down his table napkin and standing up. 'I'll go along now, Nancy, and send Vera to have hers. Don't hurry,' he added, turning to Paula and Rosalind. 'We can manage for a while yet.'

Within minutes, Vera Watts, the second Sister, pushed aside the curtain and came in. She was a plump, rosy-faced girl of about Rosalind's age and type. She greeted the newcomers cordially, but with few words, and got on briskly with her meal.

'Mrs Guthrie's O.K.,' she said to Nancy Morton. 'Some time this afternoon, I should think.'

Within twenty minutes of sitting down for lunch, or dinner as they seemed to call it here, Paula and Rosalind were following Nancy Morton to the wards.

'We have three four-bedded wards,' she said, 'but I've never seen them full; and another small one, one-bedded, for special cases. The heart case is there now. Then there is the labour ward, the nursery and the sterilising room, with the sluice, all quite close together.' She was pointing to various doors as she spoke. 'Then the kitchen is down that passage, but it's all very compact, as you can see. I haven't time to take you into the rooms now, but we'll go first to the special ward, that's Mr Lowther. I expect we'll find Doc there, but he'll be champing to get to the labour ward, I know. Have you had much experience of heart cases?'

'Well—yes, we both have,' Paula replied as they followed Sister Morton into the small one-bedded room.
She was right about Dr Renwick. He was there sitting
beside his patient, but got up as the three girls came in
and immediately said,

'Right, Sister, I'll leave it to you. I must get back to
Mrs Guthrie. She's getting the pains every two minutes,
quite strong, and everything seems all right, but in view
of her medical history I'd like to be there.' He stroked
his chin in a worried fashion. 'Come along as soon as
you're free,' and with long strides he hurried from the
room.

Sister Morton took a swift glance at the patient, a
middle-aged man, with a pale strongly-featured face and
thick, iron-grey hair. He was lying back on his pillows
with closed eyes. She studied his face for a moment, then
turned to Paula.

'I'll leave you with him,' she said softly. 'There's the
oxygen,' pointing to the long cylinder in its wheeled
stand. 'If you see the slightest change in his colour, put
the B.L.B. mask on him, wheel the cylinder close up and
give it to him. He knows what to do.'

'Where are the masks?' Paula asked, her eyes flicking
about the room. Nancy Morton pointed to the cylinder.

'It's there,' she said, 'hanging over the top, all ready
for use. All right?'

'Yes, thank you, Sister,' Paula said. 'Sorry, I didn't
notice it there at first.' She walked over and looked at the
patient. He looked comfortable, she thought, and his
colour was good.

'We can do with you in the labour ward,' she heard
Sister Morton say to Rosalind. 'Come, I'll take you
along there. Oh, by the way,' she turned back to Paula,
'if you want anything or anyone, ring the bell. There it is,
just over the patient's bed.' Rosalind turned at the door
and gave Paula a grin and a wave of the hand as she
disappeared after Nancy Morton.

Paula sat down in the chair beside the bed. The room
was very quiet, the only sound being the patient's soft,

unhurried breathing. Paula looked at him, at the bold jutting nose and firm chin. Though he looked ill, and there was a pinched, discoloured look about his lips, he was a striking-looking man, she thought. Presently she arose and walked very quietly to the window and looked out. A gardener was outside working on the flowerbeds, snipping off the wilted heads of the tulips. Across the road some children were playing on the beach.

Paula thought suddenly of Christopher Deane and wondered where he was. Perhaps he had left already. Into her mind came the memory of Bob Shaw, and his horridly significant words, and she winced inwardly. Paula had liked Christopher from the start, and she was sure that he had felt the same. Had he really read a special meaning into those words? And if so, why? Why did he have to think the worst? Was he, in spite of his pleasant looks, a narrow-minded prig? She gave a slight shrug of the shoulders. Pity it had to happen, she thought, but it'll work out some time. And if it doesn't, well, she wasn't going to let it spoil the interest and excitement of a new life in a new country.

Her thoughts moved on to the journey just completed—the apple orchards, the green ranks of fruit canes, the breath-stopping view of Hobart Harbour as seen from high up at the bend of the road, the meandering journey following the turns and twists of the River Huon, and now the glittering blue sheet of water spread out in front of her which the friendly man on the coach had told them was Esperance Bay. Paula drew a deep breath of content, then turned sharply at a slight sound behind her. It was a kind of gasp, and in a couple of strides she was there at the bed, bending over her patient. His eyes were open, and his head was turning spasmodically from side to side as if looking for someone.

'Sister!' he gasped, and clutched suddenly at his breast. Paula saw the blue ring round his mouth reached swiftly for the oxygen stand.

'It's all right, Mr Lowther,' she said quietly as she

moved it into position. His eyes turned to her, and he opened his mouth to speak, but Paula had already taken the B.L.N. mask and deftly slipped it over his nose and mouth. Swiftly but unhurriedly she clasped the mask at the back of his head, then turned the key of the cylinder. She sat down beside him and took his hand in hers as he drew the first struggling breaths. His hand gripped hers with a desperate urgency, but gradually the breathing became more even, and his fingers slackened. With relief Paula saw the blue tinge in his face fading, and a more natural colour returning to his lean cheeks. She waited quietly beside his bed and had just decided that the present crisis had passed when the door opened and Sister Morton came in. She exclaimed sharply and hurried over to the bed, looked at the patient, then turned to smile at Paula.

'He's all right now,' she said. 'How long did that attack last?'

'Just a few minutes, really,' Paula replied, 'but it seemed a long time.' She looked at the man in the bed. 'Yes, I think it's all over. I'll take off the mask. He seems comfortable.'

'Would you like a cup of tea, Mr Lowther?' Nancy Morton asked, as Paula gently raised the patient's head and unclipped the rubber mask. He blinked his eyes and smiled, showing nice, healthy-looking teeth.

'I would that,' he replied in a slightly breathless voice, then looked at Paula and back to Nancy. 'And who's this bonny wee lass?' he asked.

Nancy laughed. 'This is Sister Bruce, Mr Lowther,' she said. 'Just out from home. She's taking my place.'

'I'm verra sorry you're going, my dear,' he said earnestly, then, with a twinkle of very blue eyes, 'but if it's got to be, then I'm glad Hobart sent this one. Just the sight of her bonny face first thing in the morning will keep the old ticker going, I'm sure.' Both girls laughed, and Nancy said to Paula,

'Don't believe a word he says. The hearts Mr Lowther has broken are strewn all over Tassie. Now you're not to start chattering,' she said to him, her voice becoming serious. 'You've got to rest and stay quiet for a while. I'll go and get that tea.' She nodded to Paula and hurried out.

Mr Lowther patted the chair beside him. 'Sit down here,' he said. 'Tell me something about yourself.'

Paula did so, reminding him at the same time of what Sister Morton had said.

'I'll not say a word,' he promised, and patted her hand, and when Nancy returned with the tea he was lying back quietly listening to Paula's account of their voyage out from England.

Later that night, as they sat at supper, Nancy Morton said to Paula, 'We'll do the take-over when we've finished, and pray that no one else will come in. Mrs Guthrie's had her baby, thank heaven, with no complications. She lost her first two, rhesus negative, you know; that's why Doc Renwick was a bit worried. Mrs Jones is coming along nicely; she should produce some time tonight or early in the morning, and the other patient, Mrs Smithson, is doing nothing at all. If she doesn't start soon, I think a medical induction is indicated. But that will be up to you. She's sleeping peacefully at present. Doc Renwick is with Mr Lowther—they're old friends, by the way. So, if you've finished, shall we start? The inventory is quite a long onc. We'll start with the sterilising room.'

'Mr Lowther's a nice old chap, isn't he?' Paula observed, a few minutes later, pausing in the act of counting bedpans.

'Not so much of the old,' Nancy replied, ticking the number off on the list. 'He's not looking his best at present, poor lamb, but he's really quite a charmer, *and* the right side of fifty.'

'Fifty!' Paula echoed, and laughed. 'What does he do for a living?' She reached for a pile of kidney dishes.

'Do! He doesn't have to do anything. How many in that lot? There should be a dozen. Right?' She ticked off another time. 'Yes, our Mr Lowther is one of the richest men in Tasmania. He's also the most eligible bachelor.'

CHAPTER FIVE

PAULA's first night on duty in the hospital at Dover was fairly peaceful after the handing-over had been completed. Mr Lowther had no further attacks, and Mrs Guthrie and the new baby spent a quiet night. Mrs Jones, a frail, fair-haired girl who was expecting the arrival of her first child, rang the bell at about five a.m., and when Paula went in to see her she at once hurried the girl into the labour ward.

'She's started,' she said in a low tone to Rosalind who had followed her in, 'and I don't think it'll be a long job, either. I'll just give her a check-up.' She turned to the trolley, and taking a pair of forceps, whisked away the white linen cover. Paula ran a practised eye over the instrument container, kidney dishes, cotton wool swabs and the bowl of Dettol water, then turned to Rosalind. 'Everything O.K.' she said. 'Will you bring the gas and air machine while I scrub up and get ready?'

Rosalind hurried out, and while she was gone Paula picked up the syringe and filled it with ergometrine in readiness for the injection after the birth. She moved over to the bed and smiled down at the anxious-eyed girl. 'Nothing to worry about,' she told her. 'Everything will soon be over and your baby will be here.'

When Rosalind returned a minute later Paula had already put on the long, loose white gown over her overall and was wearing the white gauze mask over her nose and mouth. She was scrubbing her hands at the washbasin.

'Do me up, Ross,' Paula said, moving over to the trolley. She picked up the sterile towel and carefully dried her hands, then unwrapped the rubber gloves which were waiting for her on the trolley. The tiny packet of powder was also there, and after using it to ease on the gloves, Paula was ready. 'All right, Mrs Jones,' she called over her shoulder as the girl on the high, narrow bed gave a smothered gasp, 'I'm just coming,' and she moved quickly over to her side. Paula saw that the girl was looking white and scared.

'Don't worry, dear,' she said, smiling at her, 'you're doing very nicely indeed.' The patient's face was suddenly contorted with pain, and Paula glanced quickly at the clock hanging above the bed, and noted the time. 'Now,' she said, 'I want you to relax between the pains, but press down hard when you have them. Understand?' The girl nodded, then caught her breath. 'Another one?' Paula looked again at the clock; barely three minutes. 'Bring the gas and air, please,' she said, turning to Rosalind, 'and telephone Dr Renwick. Look in on Mr Lowther as you pass, but don't stay up any longer, Ross. I'll ring if I want any help.'

When Rosalind had gone Paula turned again to the girl lying on the high flat bed. She saw that she was inhaling the gas and air and already was looking much more relaxed. She moved the mouthpiece for a moment and smiled weakly at Paula.

'How'm I doing, Sister?' she whispered. Paula did a quick examination.

'Very well,' she said. 'I don't think it will be a very long labour. Go on breathing the gas and air, and press hard with every pain.' She looked across the patient at Rosalind, who was lingering at the door, and nodded. 'Now,' Paula bent over Mrs Jones, 'when I give you the word I want you to stop pressing and take just quick little breaths. Even though you may want to press hard, you must not. Understand?'

There was comparative silence in the small room. 'Now,' Paula said again, leaning towards the patient, then she paused and looked up at a sound from the door. It opened just a few inches and half of Dr Renwick's face appeared. He raised his eyebrows and Paula nodded. Without a word, he came in, put on the mask which was lying ready for him, then crossed to the basin and washed his hands. He stood bending over the trolley for a minute or two, then came over to the patient.

'She's being very quick, Doctor,' Paula said to him in a low tone. He nodded.

'Just a whiff of ether, Sister, and that's all she'll know about it,' he said, taking hold of the patient's wrist, and smiling down into her drawn face. 'Now, breathe in, Mrs Jones,' and through the room spread the sickly fumes of the anaesthetic. By eleven a.m. Master Jones had made his appearance.

'There you are,' Paula said, putting the baby into his dazed-looking mother's arms. 'Give him a little cuddle and he'll know you're his mum.' The girl stared down at the tiny crimson face with all her heart in her eyes.

'How much does he weigh, Sister?' she whispered.

'We'll weigh him after his bath. I'd say about seven pounds. Now, would you like a cup of tea?' and almost as she asked the question the door opened, and there was Rosalind with a tray in her hands. 'Come in,' Paula said, taking the baby from his mother and placing him in the cot. 'We're all ready for some refreshment. Not you,' she said to the baby as he let out a protesting cry. 'You're not ready yet, but never mind. It won't be long.'

'Let me look at him,' Rosalind said, then whispered to Paula, 'Our first Tassie baby.'

Nancy Morton now appeared to admire the new baby. She congratulated his rapidly-recovering young mother, then said to Paula, 'Come along now and have some breakfast, then Vera and I can fix up the new arrival and his mother. She'll be all right to leave for a few minutes. Feeling all right, Mrs Jones?'

'Yes, thank you, Sister.' Mrs Jones relaxed against the pillows with closed eyes, then half opened them and smiled at Paula. 'I just can't believe it's really all over,' she said.

'Wasn't so bad after all, was it?'

'Wait till it's your turn,' was the reply, and Paula

laughed with her. She took off the mask and followed Nancy from the room.

'Well, that leaves only Mrs Smithers,' said the latter a few minutes later as she poured Paula a cup of tea. 'And she's placidly knitting at present. You'd better see what Doc Renwick thinks about an induction. He's against them as a general rule.' She paused and looked at Paula. 'The coach is picking us up at ten, so things are working out rather well. There's no one else due for three days. Mrs Aust is the next, and I shouldn't think Doc will keep Mr Lowther in for long.' She glanced at her watch. 'It's now eight-thirty. I suggest you two relax while Vera and I see to Mrs Jones and the baby. No, no, we've got plenty of time,' as Paula started to protest. 'You can be looking through the case sheets and temperature charts while you're relaxing. They're in the desk over there with the appointments book.'

'Thanks,' Paula said, leaning back in her chair. 'I'm dying for a good wash and brush-up.'

'How long are you staying here?' Nancy asked, putting down her cup and standing up. 'You are Tourist, aren't you?'

'Yes, we are. Miss Needham didn't say how long,' Paula replied, and Rosalind added,

'She didn't really tell us much at all, did she, Paula?'

'No, I'm not surprised.' Nancy paused at the door. 'She's always snowed under with paper work, and usually forgets the most important things—important to us, I mean. I do know that a girl from the mainland is coming here, but whether she's permanent, and when she's due, I haven't a clue.'

'Well, I'm in no hurry to move on,' Rosalind said, laughing. 'I think I'm going to like it here.'

'And I,' Paula agreed, putting down her cup and standing up. 'Well, I'm going to shed this,' she flicked at her crumpled overall, 'and have a wash. Coming, Ross?'

By twelve o'clock, when the coach rolled up, everything in the little hospital was quiet and orderly. 'Goodbye,' Nancy said to Paula as the driver stowed the cases away at the back. 'I hope we run into you again, some-when and somewhere; and I do hope you'll be happy here.'

'We will,' Rosalind said, shaking hands in her turn, 'and the best of luck to you both. Goodbye, Vera.' Paula and Rosalind stood at the door waving till the coach turned the corner. Then they looked at each other and smiled.

'Well, here we are,' Paula said, her face flushed with excitement. 'On our own, in our own little hospital, Ross. Fun, isn't it?' She squeezed her friend suddenly round the waist.

'Lovely,' Rosalind agreed, blue eyes dancing. 'Paula, I've got a feeling that something wonderful's going to happen.'

Paula laughed. 'Come on,' she said, turning to go in. 'Dr Renwick will be here soon to do his rounds. Your something wonderful will have to wait.'

Rosalind shook her head. 'No, I really mean it,' she said, turning to follow. 'It's like something I've been waiting for without knowing it—and now it's suddenly here, just round the corner.'

On the last word a figure appeared from round the back of the hospital. It was dressed in old corduroys and a grubby faded plaid shirt. A battered hat rested on wispy grey hair and half hid a wrinkled leathery face. He grinned at the two girls.

'Y'll be the two new Sisters,' he remarked. 'What about that load o' manure?' They stared at him for a second, then Paula quickly ducked her head and shot into the hall, where she gave way to her laughter. Rosalind followed in a minute or two, grinning all over her round rosy face.

'Well!' Paula said, still laughing, 'you must have second sight, dear. He must be the "something you've been waiting for without knowing it." He came from just round the corner.'

Rosalind giggled. 'Well, I hope he goes back round the corner, and quickly,' she said.

'Oh, that was funny!' Paula said. 'But who is he, Ross, did he say?'

'Apparently he's the man who comes once a week to do the garden. He wanted to know if the manure he'd asked for had come.'

'No, it hasn't,' Paula replied, her eyes still bright with laughter. 'Nancy mentioned it, but I'd forgotten. Go and tell him we'll see about it, will you, Ross. I must see if Dr Renwick is here. We mustn't keep him waiting the first morning. You'll be with Mr Lowther, won't you?'

She turned and pushed aside the partitioning curtain as Dr Renwick appeared at the door opposite.

'Ah, there you are, Sister,' he greeted her. 'Are we all ready? How's Mrs Jones doing?'

'Very well, Doctor,' Paula replied picking up the case sheets and temperature charts which she had left ready on the desk. 'Where will you go first?'

'Ladies first. Sister Lane is with Lowther, I take it?'

'Yes.' She knew that Rosalind would be with him by now. 'He had a very good night.'

'Good.' He stroked his chin thoughtfully. 'I think I'll do an E.C.G. on him today. Let me have a look at his case sheet.' Paula held it out for him to see. 'Ah, umm—yes.' He took it and pondered it for a moment. 'Umm—light lesion with good compensation, I should imagine.' He thought a while, then, handing the sheet back, said briskly, 'Well, we'll see. Keep him well propped up all the time, Sister, and of course—no alcohol or tobacco.' Dr Renwick chuckled. 'Though he'll try to get it, the old fox, knowing that you're new. However, let's take Mrs Guthrie first. Baby's colour all right? Good, but watch it closely for the next day or two. What of Mrs Smithson?'

'She's doing nothing,' Paula told him, and added thoughtfully, 'and according to your report, she's seven days overdue.'

'Yes, I know,' he replied a trifle testily. 'But she's having no pain or discomfort. It's a first baby, Sister, and as you know, they can be unpredictable either way.

We'll give her another day, and then if nothing happens I'll give her a med. stim.'

And so the day which was soon to become familiar routine wore smoothly and pleasantly to its close. Mr Lowther's condition was so satisfactory that he could now be left, with instructions to ring his bell if necessary. The two mothers and their babies were asleep, and Mrs Smithson was still knitting. 'It's a jolly good thing this baby's late,' she had said to Rosalind when the latter had carried in her supper tray, 'I haven't nearly finished his trousseau.'

At about nine o'clock the two girls sat down, one on either side of a wood fire, with a pot of tea between them. Paula looked out of the window to where she could just glimpse the wine-dark sea. She drew a long sigh of content, then turned to Rosalind who was pouring out the tea. 'I don't know what nurses would do without their eternal pots of tea,' she remarked.

'That heart case is rather a pet, isn't he?' Rosalind sat down and stirred her tea.

'Yes, he's nice,' Paula said. 'A rich old bachelor, too, so Nancy told me. Ross,' she stopped for a moment, 'are you going to write to Jack Sinclair?'

'Write to Jack Sinclair? Whatever for?' Rosalind looked at Paula in surprise.

'Well—' Paula's face reddened slightly, 'to thank him, I mean, for the evening out.'

'Oh, I see.' Rosalind glanced at her quickly. 'I suppose it would be only polite. Have you written—to our Mr Deane?'

Paula laughed. 'Not yet,' she said. 'Hasn't been much time, has there? But now—well?'

'Yes, I think we should,' Rosalind said, grinning. 'I'm glad you reminded me. Let's do it now, during the lull; we don't know how long it will last.'

'Ross,' Paula said a few minutes later, as she addressed the envelope on her knee to the Department of Health, Hobart, 'Nancy was telling me today how they arrange the duties. Apparently it's not considered necessary for anyone to stay up nights. We just take turns to be on call, and the one on call is off duty at midday. Nancy said it worked very well. As for days off, we have to take them at slack periods. Sometimes, you see, there'll be no one in at all, and then it's possible for one of us to have a couple of days off in Hobart.'

'Gosh, what a change from dear old St Just's,' Rosalind remarked. 'We're practically our own mistresses here.'

'With a lot of responsibility resting on us,' Paula said seriously. She paused, then added, 'Tonight I'll be on call, if that's all right with you.'

'But you've done the lion's share today,' Rosalind protested. 'Are you sure—'

'Yes, I'm not sleepy, and I'd like to do the first night, as I'm technically in charge,' Paula said. 'You get off to bed when you like, Ross, but I'll stay up for a couple of hours. O.K.?'

'Uh-huh. There are drawbacks in a job like this.' Rosalind's tone was thoughtful as she poured another cup of tea. 'We shan't get out much together, shall we?'

'Oh, it won't be too bad,' Paula replied. 'Dr Renwick's wife is an ex-Sister, you know, and Nancy said she's an awfully good sort, always ready to stand in in an emergency. She said she often came in of an evening so that she and Vera could go out together.'

'Yes, I met Mrs Renwick last night. She seems a good type. We must certainly cultivate her.' Rosalind said, yawning. She put down her cup and got up. 'Well, I'll be off to bed while the going's good. Ring if you want me, won't you?'

'I will.' Paula smiled. 'Goodnight, Ross. Not regretting it, are you?'

'No, not for one moment. I'm loving it all.' Her voice was so definite that Paula's tiny twinge of anxiety vanished. Left to herself, she picked up a magazine, but her attention soon wandered. She rose and went over to the window. The silent dark sheet of water outside took her thoughts back to Hobart—and the party at Wrest

Point. It had started so well, Paula thought regretfully, watching a moving light far out at sea. She recalled Christopher Deane's words as he had stood beside her at another window looking out on to the wide sweep of Sandy Bay. 'There are many beauty spots round here,' he had said. 'I would like to show you some, if I may. Dover is not so far off.' Paula sighed and wondered where he was now. On the mainland, perhaps. She turned away and her eyes fell on the letter she had just written. Would he reply to it? She shrugged her shoulders, and decided to make another pot of tea.

Life here is going to be very different from St Just's, Paula thought, looking round the small kitchen. She crossed to the sink and started to fill the kettle. Ordered regimentation on the one hand; it had to be, of course, in a huge training hospital; and something more like a private nursing home on the other. But it's going to be fun, she thought, a smile curving her lips; a bit like running one's own home. Paula had met Minnie, the domestic, earlier on, and the latter had informed her that Sister usually started the breakfasts in the morning, as she couldn't get to the hospital before eight. Paula washed the two cups under the tap and set one out again on the tray. She was looking for the tea caddy when the door opened quietly and a woman appeared. Paula looked at her in surprise. She was thin-faced and tired-looking, and was carrying a small case.

'Hello, Sister,' the woman said. 'I've come in. Sister Morton told me to.'

'Good evening,' Paula said. 'Are you—a patient?' Stupid question, she thought as soon as the words were spoken; one had only to look at her.

'Yes, I'm Mrs Aust. Didn't Sister Morton tell you? I suppose you're the new one. This is my fourth.'

'Yes, of course,' Paula said quickly. 'I remember now—but you're a bit early, aren't you? Would you like a cup of tea before—?'

'Well, I don't think really I've got time for it, Sister.'

'In that case,' Paula said, setting down the teapot,

'you'd better come along with me.' She took the case from Mrs Aust and turned towards the door. 'How did you get here?'

'Walked. We're a mile the other side of the village, and no neighbours.'

'You walked! By yourself? But where's your husband?' They had arrived by now at the nearest empty ward.

'He's at home with the kids,' Mrs Aust replied, hanging her coat up behind the door in a business-like fashion. 'He couldn't leave them at this time o' night. Where d'you want me, Sister—here?' and she plumped down on to the nearest bed.

'You'd better get your things off,' Paula said, 'and we'll see how far on you are.'

The woman gave a sudden lurch and fell back on to the pillows. 'It's coming,' she announced calmly, and drew a deep breath. One glance showed the horrified Paula that she was right. Oh, lord, she thought as she rang the bell, I hope Ross isn't asleep yet. Hurriedly she started to undress the patient, one eye on the door, and within two minutes Rosalind appeared. She took in the situation at a glance. No time to get the patient into the labour ward. She was back almost at once wheeling the loaded trolley.

'I'll stay with her while you get ready,' she said rapidly to Paula. 'This one won't want gas and air.'

'No, I'm the one that'll want it,' Paula gasped. 'I'll be as quick as I can, and then you must phone Dr Renwick.' She was gowned and masked in a minute, then casting a quick eye at Mrs Aust, she added, 'Stay while I scrub up,' and dashed over to the washbasin.

'That was a quick change, Sister,' remarked the patient conversationally. 'Ooh—off we go again!' She screwed up her face and half-closed her eyes, then gave a long half-sigh, half-groan. 'That's made it!' she gasped.

'You're right,' Paula agreed weakly a second later, 'and here's your daughter, Mrs Aust. Have all your family been like this one?—in such a hurry, I mean.'

'Yes,' the patient said cheerfully. 'Like shelling peas

out of a pod, they are; just can't wait.' She gave a sigh of content. 'Well, I'll get a good night's rest for once. Let's 'ave a look at 'er, Sister. Umm, like 'er dad, poor little b——'

'She's a dear little girl,' Paula said. 'Don't you want to hold her?'

'Well, just for a minute, but I could do with that cup o' tea now. Should be still hot, shouldn't it? Shame to waste it.'

Paula laughed and pushed back the damp hair from her forehead. 'That's the quickest job I've ever done,' she remarked. 'I'll see about that tea, Mrs Aust, if you're all right.' She went to the door and was met by Dr Renwick. 'I'm sorry,' Paula said to him. 'It's all over, and—' but he interrupted her with a grin.

'Never mind, Sister,' he said. 'We should have warned you about Mrs Aust. Everything all right? What's she got this time? Right. I'll just go in and have a word with her. Oh, and by the way, Mrs Smithson has started. Sister Lane's seeing to her.'

Within two weeks Paula and Rosalind had settled down in the little hospital at Dover. No more patients came in; all the mothers and babies went home, and Mr Lowther was left as the only patient.

One morning Dr Renwick said to Paula, 'Now's the time to relax, my dear. One of you should take some time off. There are no patients due for a week, so seize the opportunity. Go to Hobart for a couple of days. Do you good.' Paula sought out Rosalind, and found her with their one and only patient. He was up now and sitting at the window.

'Ah, here's my little sprig of apple-blossom,' Mr Lowther said as Paula came in, and she found herself frowning. His descriptive words made her think of Bob Shaw; and Paula did not want to think of Bob. For that very morning she had had a letter from him, forwarded from the Department of Health, Hobart. With a cold little feeling of shock she had recognised the handwriting—and remembered that a few short months ago she had thrilled to the sight of it, not shrunk away as she was doing now. Slowly and with reluctance Paula had opened the letter—and read it with rising anger and apprehension.

CHAPTER SIX

'Is anything wrong?' Rosalind asked as she followed Paula out of Mr Lowther's room. 'You look worried.'

'Yes, I am, rather. Come along to my room for a minute. I've got something to show you. Read that,' Paula added a minute later as, having closed the door behind her, she took Bob's letter from her overall pocket and handed it to Rosalind. There was silence for a minute or two.

'Well!' Rosalind said at last, and stared at Paula in consternation. 'It looks as if our friend Bob is going to be a nuisance. What are you going to do?'

Paula took the letter and stood staring down at it in silence. She looked worried.

'I've been thinking, Ross,' she said at last. 'I told you that I wanted to have nothing more to do with Bob, and I meant it. Well, he mustn't find out where I am. This, as you see, has been forwarded from the Department of Health at Hobart, and was probably posted just before his ship sailed. Tankers never stay in port for more than a day or two. But you see he says that they'll be calling in again on their way home, and I'm afraid he's determined to see me if possible. Well, I must be prepared. He may go, or write, for my address, d'you see?'

Rosalind nodded. 'Of course,' she said, then added quickly, 'Paula, you must see Miss Needham, and as soon as possible. Look, we're quiet at present. Couldn't you—'

'That's just what I was coming to.' Paula pushed the letter back into her pocket. 'Dr Renwick says one of us should take time off, so I wondered, Ross, if you'd mind if I took the first turn. I could see Miss Needham, perhaps, today, and return tomorrow.'

'Why, of course. You do that. Look, go and pack a

case now, and I'll telephone for the coach to pick you up. You've just got time if you hurry.'

'Thanks, Ross,' Paula said gratefully. 'I hoped you'd say that. The sooner this business is settled the better. Do the same for you one day.'

'I hope not,' Rosalind laughed. 'Go on, hurry!'

Within the half-hour Paula was settled in the coach and on her way to Hobart. In spite of the nagging worry about the letter in her handbag, she enjoyed the journey. The apple-trees were no longer in bloom, and Paula was interested to notice that the sprayers were already at work. She caught her breath with delight again at the perfect view of Hobart Harbour, but as the coach started the descent into the town her thoughts turned to the coming interview with Miss Needham, an interview she was not looking forward to at all.

The coach arrived just before lunch-time, and Paula went straight to Davey Street. Get it over as soon as possible, she thought. Miss Needham was, as usual, sitting behind stacks of papers and files. She looked up from her desk as Paula was shown in.

'Hello, my dear,' she said. 'Having a little well-earned rest? What can I do for you?'

Paula walked towards her. 'Good morning, Miss Needham,' she said, smiling a trifle nervously. 'Yes, we're having a quiet time just now, so—' she hesitated.

'Of course, why not?' Miss Needham interrupted briskly. 'Staying at McQuarrie Street, are you?'

'Just for the night,' Paula said. 'Er—Miss Needham, there's something I want to ask you, if you can spare a moment.'

'Of course. Sit down, my dear. Now, what's the trouble? Nothing gone wrong, I hope?'

'No, no, nothing wrong,' Paula said, pulling a chair forward. 'It's a—personal matter. You forwarded a letter to me. I got it this morning. I—well, it was from someone to whom I was once engaged. The engagement was broken off—by him. But now he's trying to start it all over again. I don't want this. It's all over as far as I'm concerned, and I have no wish to see or hear from him again, so—' She stopped and looked, with flushed cheeks, at Miss Needham.

The latter nodded. 'Have you told the young man all this?' she asked.

'Yes, I have. He's away on his ship now, but it will be coming back to Hobart.'

'I see.' Miss Needham looked thoughtful. 'And you think he may call here and ask for your address?' Paula nodded. 'Well, set your mind at rest, my dear. We never give addresses, only forward letters that come here. So you have nothing to worry about on that score. Just ignore any further letters. If any come, we'll have to send them on, of course, but—is he likely to stay in Hobart?'

'No, thank goodness,' Paula replied. 'He's a radio officer on a tanker. The ship called in a few weeks ago, and he says in this letter that they will be calling back, and that he wants to see me. But tankers only stay for a day or two at the most.'

Miss Needham smiled reassuringly at Paula's embarrassed face. 'Well, that's all right, then,' she said. 'He won't get the address from me, or from the club; and he won't be here long enough to find you. Put it right out of your mind, my dear. Now, what about some lunch? Come and have some with me.'

'Thank you very much,' Paula said, lighthearted again now that this uncomfortable interview was over. 'I'd love that.'

'Right. We'll go now while the going's good. Come along.' Miss Needham took Paula to a little restaurant "just round the corner," where she spent a most entertaining half-hour listening to the latter's stories of bush nursing in the outback of Australia. Indeed, so absorbed did Paula become that when Miss Needham stood up to go, she said impulsively,

'Could you—would you have supper with me tonight, Miss Needham? I'm dying to hear more about the Australian Inland Missions.'

'I'll be pleased to,' was the hearty reply. 'But, instead of going out, you come along to my flat, and we'll have something there. I've got some photographs which I think you'd like to see. Call for me at the office at six. Right?'

Paula strolled along to the Nurses' Club in McQuarrie Street and booked in for the night. She was feeling very much happier now; and after washing and powdering her face, she went out again, found Elizabeth Street and spent a happy couple of hours shop-gazing. After a cup of tea at a little café down by the harbour, Paula returned to the Club to make ready for her visit to Miss Needham's flat. But as she came in at the main entrance, Club Sister hurried forward to meet her. She looked worried.

'Oh, Miss Bruce,' she began, 'I wonder if you can help us out in an emergency. I've had a call from the hospital. The night Sister in charge of a special case has been taken ill. They're very short-handed at present, and have no one they can put on in her place. The day Sister on the case has offered to carry on if someone can relieve her for a couple of hours, say from ten to twelve. Well—' she looked at Paula uncertainly, then went on, 'they asked me if—well, I wondered, as you were here if— anyway, I said I would ask you. They can fix you up with uniform. I know it seems a shame on your time off, and I've never known them to ask before, but—'

'Yes, of course,' Paula said, breaking in on the rather rambling recital. 'I'll be pleased to help out. Ten to twelve, did you say? I'll go on at nine. Two hours off isn't much after being on all day.' Club Sister smiled gratefully.

'That's very good of you,' she said. 'I'll go and ring them back right away, and tell them you'll be there at nine. Thanks again,' and she hurried off to the telephone.

Paula walked upstairs to her room. There was a half-smile on her lips, and an added sparkle in her eyes. It had occurred to her while Club Sister was talking that if this special case happened to be a surgical one, then she might, just *might* meet Christopher Deane again. Though Paula had had no reply to her polite little letter of thanks for the evening at Wrest Point, Rosalind had had a cheery little screed from Jack Sinclair, in the course of which he had mentioned Christopher. So that Paula knew he was back in Hobart. There's just a chance, she thought now, laying down her handbag and preparing to tidy up; though it might not be his case, of course. She looked at her watch and saw that she would have to hurry if she was to meet Miss Needham at six. In a few minutes Paula was ready, and picking up her old handbag that had accompanied her from England, she hurried off to Davey Street.

Miss Needham frowned when on the way to her flat Paula told her of her emergency job that evening.

'I've never known that to happen before,' she remarked, stopping before the door of a tall, narrow house and taking a key from her handbag. 'It certainly must be an emergency. But it's too bad on your time off, too.'

'Oh, I don't really mind,' Paula hastened to say, and blushing for no apparent reason. 'I shall probably quite enjoy it, meeting some of the staff. I'm wondering if the Matron who interviewed us at Tasmania House in London will be there.' Miss Needham shook her head as she led the way in and up some stairs.

'That would be Miss Norris,' she remarked. 'She's at the Royal Hobart, but she's not back from home yet.'

'Pity, I'd like to have met her again.'

'Oh, you will,' Miss Needham assured her. 'She makes a point of knowing all the Tourist nursing staff as well as the permanent people. Sit down and make yourself at home while I get some things from the fridge.'

'It's a special case I've been asked to help with,' Paula said a few minutes later as she took her place at the table opposite Miss Needham, then added rather self-consciously, 'probably surgical, don't you think?'

'Not necessarily,' was the disappointing answer.

'Could be anything. Have some salad.'

'Thank you. I expect I shall be just sitting in. The doctor, physician or surgeon, whichever he is, isn't likely to call at such a time.' Paula waited, her eyes on her plate.

'I don't know what the routine is,' Miss Needham replied. 'Do have another tomato; I grew them myself. You were asking me at lunch-time about the A.I.M. Well, I've got some fine photographs of Darwin and Cloncurry to show you. We'll look at them over coffee. It's a pity you have to go so early. If ever you thought of going over to the mainland, I could—' and so the talk drifted far away from the Royal Hospital, Hobart, and Christopher Deane, F.R.C.S.

Just before nine Paula presented herself at the inquiry office of the huge hospital in Liverpool Street. She had stared at the building with surprised interest as she walked up the broad drive. It was not the size; Paula had been in large hospitals before. It was the design—more like an enormous white block of flats, she had thought, and decided that she liked it in spite of its strangeness. The whole building was flood-lit and looked most impressive. Paula was taken up in a lift, along several long corridors, and eventually into a vast ward with a neat double row of white cots stretching into the distance. Day Sister of the special case came out from a small side room and greeted Paula. She looked pale and jaded.

'Good evening, Sister Bruce,' she said. 'It's very good of you to come along. This is the men's medical ward.' Paula's heart sank. 'But the special,' she beckoned Paula to follow her into the small room, 'is a surgical case. This was the only room available.' Paula's heart regained its normal position as Sister Ferguson crossed over to the bed. 'The sphyg. is here,' Sister pointed to a case on the side table. 'And here is the report. As you will see, the pulse and temperature are steady and the general condition of the patient is satisfactory. Now, I'll get Staff Nurse to take you to the changing room. You'll find everything you'll want. I'll wait here till you get back.'

Within five minutes the change-over was effected and Paula was installed in the small room with the special case. She read the report carefully. 'Road accident. Concussion. Severe head injuries,' then walked softly over to the bed to look at the patient. The head and most of the face was completely hidden by bandages, but she noted that he was sleeping peacefully and his breathing was quiet and regular. Paula noticed that the water jug on the side table was more than half empty, so, picking it up, she opened the door leading into the large ward and beckoned to the staff nurse, a bright young thing of about twenty. When the girl returned with the full jug, she smiled at Paula in a friendly fashion and remarked,

'You're one of the Tourist Service, aren't you, Sister?'

Paula looked down the long ward. Night Sister was busily writing in a screened-off enclosure at the other end. Her own special was peacefully asleep, and there was not a sound from the other patients. She smiled at Nurse Rogers and nodded.

'That's what I'm going to do when I've finished my training,' said the latter. 'I like getting about and seeing places. How is he?' she nodded towards the half-closed door behind Paula.

'Very satisfactory,' Paula replied. 'Do you know if the surgeon is likely to be in tonight?'

'Oh, I shouldn't think so, Sister. He was in at six, and I heard him tell Sister Ferguson that he was very pleased with the patient.'

'I see. That would be Mr Deane, wouldn't it?' Paula waited eagerly for the answer.

'Well, I don't know the names very well, not the surgeons'. This is really men's medical, you see.'

'Yes, of course,' Paula murmured. 'Well, I must be getting back. Thanks for bringing the water.' Serves me right, she thought, closing the door behind her, I shouldn't have tried to pump the girl.

Paula crossed over and took another careful look at her patient. He had drawn one arm from under the bedclothes, and it was folded across his breast. She placed her fingers gently on the wrist, satisfied herself that his pulse was normal and steady, then very carefully replaced the limb under the covers.

Everything was very quiet. The whole hospital seemed asleep. Paula glanced at her watch. Ten-thirty. She walked over to the window and looked down into brightly lit Liverpool Street. Other well-illuminated streets intersected it at right angles, and still others from those. She looked straight ahead and could pick out the ships in the harbour. The scene recalled to Paula her evening at Wrest Point—her first evening in Hobart. It had started so happily, and ended full of frustration. But it's not the end, Paula suddenly thought, I know it's not.

She looked round for something to employ her time, and saw a copy of *The Lancet* on a shelf. She opened it at an article on brain surgery, and after reading a few lines, sat down with it by the patient's bed. So engrossed did Paula become that she did not hear the almost noiseless opening of the door.

'Good evening, Sister,' said a quiet voice. 'How is—' then it stopped as Paula raised her head and looked at him. 'You! But what are *you* doing here?'

Paula rose quickly to her feet, bright colour flooding her cheeks.

'Good evening, sir,' she said. 'I—' and then she told Christopher Deane how she came to be there in temporary charge of his case.

'I see,' he said briefly, and turned to look at the figure on the bed. 'May I see the report, Sister?' The flush faded from Paula's face as she handed it to him. 'How is he?'

'Everything is quite satisfactory, Mr Deane,' she said. 'His condition, since I took over, has remained the same.'

'Good. Good.' He bent closely over the patient, and watched the calm face for a full minute before straightening himself with a satisfied sigh.

'How are you liking Tasmania?' he asked suddenly, turning to look at Paula. Her heart took a quick lift.

'I love it,' she said, her lips curving up in their ready smile. 'It's—it's a beautiful country. I'm spending two days in Hobart,' she added, and waited.

'Quiet at Dover, eh?'

Paula nodded and waited again.

'Yes, that's the way it goes,' he said, carefully placing the report back on the table. 'We're up to our eyes in it just now, but next week it's quite likely that we shall be half empty. One never can look ahead in our line of business.' He smiled briefly at Paula and continued. 'Now last month we had—'

Paula took a furtive look at her watch. A quarter to twelve. Sister Ferguson would be back soon. Oh, why did Christopher have to go on in this awful impersonal way? What could she say to him to—? The door quietly opened and Sister Ferguson came in.

'Good evening, Mr Deane,' she said, and smiled. 'I expect you're surprised to see so many strangers here tonight.'

He smiled at her and moved in the direction of the door.

'Yes, but Sister Bruce has explained.' At least he remembers my name, Paula thought. 'I've seen the patient, and now I must see Mrs Wragg, in women's surgical. Goodnight, Sister.' He included them both in a half-nod, half-bow, and hurried off.

'Well, that's that,' said Sister Ferguson. 'This has been a great help,' she added, turning to Paula. 'Anything to report? No? Right, you hurry off now and get changed. I'll order some transport to take you back to the Club.'

'Oh, no, please don't bother,' Paula said quickly. 'Er—that's all right. A—a friend is taking me back.' She blushed guiltily as she met the other girl's surprised eye. Well, Christopher *was* a friend, or had been; and Paula had plans to make him one again. 'Goodnight, Sister,' she said, and hurried off to the changing room.

Rapidly Paula shed her white uniform and slipped her frock over her head. She drew a quick comb through her dark hair, and picked up her handbag. Within minutes she was down at the big entrance hall. There she took a quick glance round. There was no one about. Paula waited. Then, as she heard the sound of the descending lift, she pushed open the door and walked slowly down the broad flight of stone steps. Out of the corner of her eye Paula saw the door open behind her, and then she heard his voice.

'Er—Paula—Miss Bruce.' Her heart exulted. So he remembered her first name too. 'Wait a moment. Can I offer you a lift?' Paula looked at him over her shoulder and hesitated. 'Why haven't you got transport? I would have offered before, but—'

'Thank you,' Paula said, stopping and waiting for him. 'I—er—it's not far to the Club. I don't want to take you out of your way.'

'Oh, but it's on my way,' Christopher replied, taking her by the elbow and leading her towards the car which Paula had already noted waiting at the kerb. He helped her in, then went round to the other side and got in beside her. There was silence for a second or two. This is your chance, Paula was telling herself. Don't waste it; you'll be at the Club in a minute or two.

'I—' she began at the same moment as he started to speak. They both waited, then laughed together.

'You were going to say—?' He waited. Paula looked at his profile uncertainly. He looks very composed, she thought. Perhaps he has forgotten all about Bob and the incident at Wrest Point Hotel. Perhaps—then she rallied herself.

'Mr Deane, there's—something I wanted to say—' He turned and looked at her in surprise and a painful blush rushed up into Paula's cheeks. This is awful, she thought, he's giving me no help at all. Perhaps he *has* forgotten. But suddenly Christopher smiled.

'I wanted to say something, too,' he said. 'I wanted to thank you for your letter. Now it's your turn. What was it you were going to say?'

Paula felt the car slowing down and knew that they were outside the Club already. The car stopped, and the light from a street lamp fell full on Paula's flushed face.

'Come,' Christopher said suddenly, 'I'll see you to the door,' and got out.

Oh, good! Paula thought thankfully, as she waited for him to open the door on her side. It's dark under the porch; I can say it better there. But as she stepped out of the car, it happened. Fumblingly she had picked up her handbag. But, as she ducked her head to climb out, it slipped from her fingers and fell on the pavement, spilling its contents at Christopher's feet. He bent forward at the same moment as Paula, and for a moment their faces almost touched. He made a sudden movement forward, and for one breathless moment Paula thought—but quickly he drew back, and started to gather up the assortment of articles scattered on the pavement.

'Oh, I am sorry,' Paula muttered, flustered yet excited at the same time. Hurriedly she bent again to help him, then stopped, her eyes widening in dismay. There, a little apart from the rest of the contents of the bag, was the old photograph of Bob which she had pushed into this handbag months ago. How had it remained there so long? Paula wondered unhappily. Stuck in one of the many flaps, she supposed. Anyway, there it was; creased a little, certainly, but with the smiling face quite clear and easily recognisable. She reached out a swift hand to pick it up, but Christopher was before her.

'I'm sure you won't want to lose this,' he said, holding it out, and Paula wondered if it were an accident that his thumb seemed to be pointing to the words scrawled at the bottom of the photograph in large bold letters, 'To my darling Paula, with all my love. Bob.' She met the level grey glance of his eyes, and faltered.

'Oh, it doesn't matter,' she said hurriedly, taking the picture from him and pushing it into the bag again. 'It's—it's just an old thing. I'd forgotten I still had it.'

'Really!' Christopher said. 'Surprising.' He picked up a comb and handed it to her. 'But doubtless you have others.'

'Why is it so surprising?' Paula asked, her eyes beginning to snap. She looked straight at him, and he returned the glance.

'Well,' he said, 'I rather got the impression on our one and only evening out that this young man was rather a—special friend.'

Paula took an eager step forward. 'But that's just what I wanted to tell you about,' she said. 'I wanted to explain.'

He smiled in a maddening way. 'But there's nothing really to explain, is there?' he said. 'I quite understood.' He took a step away from her.

'Did you?' Paula said in a slightly trembling voice. 'Then I won't bore you with my explanation as you've so obviously supplied one of your own. Goodnight, Mr Deane, and thank you for the lift.' And clutching the fateful handbag to her, Paula disappeared into the porch of the Nurses' Club.

CHAPTER SEVEN

PAULA sat in the coach on her way back to Dover. She gazed out at the apple orchards which were now green instead of pink and white. But this time, instead of noting every fresh scene with lively interest, she hardly saw them at all, for her thoughts were turned inwards upon herself.

She was thinking of the events of the previous night. Christopher had recognised Bob's face in the photograph at once. That had been obvious. Paula's face flushed as she recalled his sarcastic remark as he handed it to her. And then his further comments. But perhaps he hadn't meant to be sarcastic. And then she had lost her temper. He had looked so—so superior, somehow. But she wished now that she hadn't; though perhaps one good thing had come of it, Paula thought. At least she knew now that he was not indifferent. His words showed that he had been annoyed, even hurt perhaps, at her seeming desertion of him for Bob at Wrest Point. Paula sighed and wished she hadn't rushed off just when she did; she'd only made things worse. Yet had she?

Her hazel eyes stared out unseeing at the passing landscape—and then the wide mouth began to twitch at the corners. Perhaps not. She had at least put a doubt into his mind, surely. Sometime he would remember what Paula had said about wanting to explain; that there was something she wanted to tell him. Her lips broke into a smile which spread to her eyes. Yes, Paula decided, she'd at least given Christopher something to think about. This was not the end of it, she felt.

'Did you fix it up with Miss Needham?' Rosalind asked a few hours later as the two girls sat together over lunch. She regarded Paula anxiously. There was about her a slightly harassed air which in Paula was unusual.

'Yes, I did.' She looked down at her plate as she spoke.

'Good. Well, apart from that, did you have a good time?'

'Yes, quite. I had lunch with Miss Needham, and in the evening had supper at her flat. But for the rest—well, it was a bit of a busman's holiday,' and Paula told Rosalind about the three hours' "stand-in" at the Hobart Hospital.

'Gosh, that must have been interesting,' she said. 'Did you have much to do?'

'No, nothing really. It was a surgical case.' She looked across the table. 'Mr Deane's patient.'

'Really, Paula! And did you see anything of him while you were there?'

'Yes.' She stopped, then decided to tell the whole story to Rosalind. 'As a matter of fact, he drove me back to the Club. But don't get any wrong ideas about that. We parted on very strained terms.'

'Go on, tell me all,' Rosalind said; and at the end of the recital, 'What an idiot you were to lose your temper like that, Paula. After meeting up with him again, too, *and* at such a propitious time. That miserable Bob seems to be always throwing spanners in your works. Do you think that Christopher *really* thinks—'

'I don't know what he thinks,' Paula interrupted, rising from the table. 'Your guess is as good as mine. Perhaps he's not interested. After all, why should he be? I only met him for one day, and I'm not conceited enough to think that—'

'Oh, yes, you are,' Rosalind cut in briskly, pushing back her chair.

Paula looked at her and laughed. 'Ross, you are a beast,' she said. 'Well, that's that, for the moment, anyway. What's the position here? Mr Lowther still in?'

'Yes, but he goes tomorrow. There's a Mrs Jenkins almost due. Paula,' Rosalind's eyes were bright, 'Mr Lowther's asked us to a big New Year's party at his house.'

'Nice of him,' Paula said. 'But we can't both go. You go, Ross, it's your turn.' Rosalind grinned at her in triumph.

'But we can both go,' she said. 'That is, if it's quiet here, as it probably will be. After all, no one who doesn't have to would spend New Year's Eve in a hospital bed. Listen, Paula. Dr Renwick has said that if there are only one or two patients in, and nothing pending, he and Mrs Renwick will come here and stay while we go to the party.'

Paula looked at her thoughtfully. 'Well, it's jolly good of them,' she said at last, 'but do you think we ought to?'

Rosalind made an impatient gesture. 'Doc wouldn't suggest it if it weren't all right,' she said. 'He says it's the party of the year.'

'All right, then. We'll just have to hope that it's quiet here at New Year.'

The next two weeks passed quietly and uneventfully. There were one or two minor accident cases; and then, one morning, just before midday dinner, Mrs Aust arrived, pushing her baby in a pram. Two toddlers clutched at her skirts.

'Hello, Sister,' she greeted Paula. 'I've brought young Sandra back. She don't seem to be getting on at all. Thought you'd better 'ave a look at 'er.' She lifted the baby from the pram.

'Come and sit down,' Paula said, taking the baby from her. 'What's the trouble?'

'Well, Sister, she's always grizzling.'

'Does she take her feeds all right?' Paula sat down with the baby in her lap, and unwrapped its shawl.

'Oh, yes, Sister, she's always ready for that; but she seems to get tired, and then drops off in the middle of it. Then in a couple of hours or less, she's awake again, grizzling.'

Paula handed the child to her mother and brought out the baby scales. 'I'll weigh her,' she said. 'Eight pounds, three ounces when she went out, wasn't it? Well, let's see how much she's gained.' She spread a clean cloth

over the scales, then took the baby and rapidly undressed her to the tiny vest and nappy. Sandra raised a
yell as Paula placed her on the scales. 'All right, all
right,' she said. 'Nothing wrong with your lungs, anyway.' She bent over the scales. 'Thought so,' she said,
turning to Mrs Aust. 'She's gained barely two ounces
since she went out. She's not getting nearly enough. All
right, Sandra,' she said, picking up the still yelling child,
and wrapping her in the shawl.

'Now, Mrs Aust,' Paula said, 'I want you to feed her;
it's almost time, isn't it? Give her as much as she'll take
and then I'll weigh her again, and we'll be able to see just
how much she's had. Right.'

While Paula was talking she heard Rosalind's voice
from the hall. She appeared to be talking on the telephone. A patient coming in, perhaps, Paula thought,
and then heard Rosalind laugh.

'Well, I'm keeping my fingers crossed,' she heard her
say. 'We both are.' One of Mrs Aust's toddlers began to
pull impatiently at his mother's arm, and Paula went to
the cupboard and opened it. 'Look,' she said, turning
round with a rather battered-looking train and a limp
teddy bear in her arms, 'wouldn't you like to play with
these?' They were kept in the cupboard for just such a
purpose. 'Mummy's not quite ready yet.' The two
looked at the toys just as Sandra let out an angry shriek.

'She won't take any more,' said her worried-looking
mother, 'but it's not enough, is it, Sister?'

'Perhaps there's no more to have,' Paula suggested.
'Let's see,' and she took the child and placed her again
on the scales. 'I don't wonder she's angry,' she said,
turning to Mrs Aust. 'The poor lamb's had barely two
ounces. You obviously haven't enough for her.'

'But the others were all right,' Mrs Aust protested. 'I
fed them all for six months. Why—'

'Don't worry,' Paula said. 'You're doing too much, I
expect. Probably work yourself to a standstill, don't
you? You just can't do everything, you know.'

'Well, I 'ave got plenty to do, Sister, but then I've

always done it. Well—' she looked helplessly at Paula, 'what am I going to do?'

Paula smiled and handed the baby back to her. 'Supplement her feeds, of course,' she said. 'Look,' she went to the cupboard and reached to the top shelf, 'we'll give her some "afters" right away.' Paula brought the tin to the table. 'I'll mix a feed for her now, and you must give her at least another two ounces after every feed in future. The instructions are on the tin, and I want you to bring her up again in a couple of days for me to weigh. Come on, Sandra, here's something you'll really like.' Within ten minutes Mrs Aust, the two toddlers, and a peacefully-sleeping baby had disappeared up the drive. Paula went in search of Rosalind and found her in the garden.

'Mrs Aust's been in with Sandra,' she said. 'Who were you talking to on the phone?'

Rosalind stared dreamily out at the yellow beach and blue sea just across the road. 'That was Angus Lowther,' she said. 'He wanted to know if we are all set for the party. It's only a week off, Paula. Oh, I do hope we can go, don't you?'

Paula was looking up the road. 'Yes, rather,' she replied rather absently. 'Look, Ross,' as a figure on a bicycle rounded the bend, 'here's the postman. It's Christmas Eve tomorrow, you know, and we should get bags of mail. I can hardly realise it.' She motioned towards the beach, 'All this lovely sun, people bathing on the beach, gardens full of flowers—and it's Christmas!'

Rosalind laughed and linked a hand in Paula's arm. 'Come and collect our Christmas mail,' she said.

'Lots of parcels for you,' the friendly postman said, turning them out of his bag. 'And letters for you both.'

'Here's one from Mummy,' Rosalind said, as they both went in to dinner. 'And a parcel; and there's one for you, too. What else have you got, Paula?'

'Long letter from Uncle. Heaps of cards—' Paula stopped and stared at a large square envelope. 'Oh, here's one with the Hobart postmark. Miss Needham, perhaps.'

Rosalind looked up curiously from the parcel she was opening. 'Well, is it?' she asked.

Bright colour crept into Paula's cheeks as she looked at the open Christmas card in her hand. Silently she passed it across for Rosalind to see. It was quite plain and formal in character, and inside it briefly said, 'To Paula, wishing you a very Happy Christmas, from Christopher Deane.'

Rosalind handed it back and turned to her own mail. 'Well, at least he hasn't forgotten you,' she said. 'Did you send him one?'

'No.' Paula seemed about to say something further, then changed her mind. 'I wonder when Mrs Jenkins is coming along,' she mused.

'She's a week overdue,' Rosalind remarked, opening another envelope, 'but it's a first, so she might hang on till after New Year's Eve.'

'Of course, if she came in now, it would be just as good,' Paula pointed out, smoothing and folding some wrapping paper. 'That's if she's the only one in, I mean.' As she spoke there was a prolonged ring at the front door bell and then Minnie's footsteps hurrying across the hall.

'Here we go,' Rosalind said, gathering up parcels and letters. 'This will be Mrs Jenkins. Cheers!'

'There's someone at the back door, too,' Paula said, listening.

Minnie's head appeared round the curtain. 'Mr Jenkins has brought her along,' she announced. 'And the gardener's at the back door with a duck.'

The two girls stared at her, then Rosalind said, 'Shall I go and see to Mrs Jenkins, as I booked her? They called while you were away, Paula. You go and see what the duck wants.'

'Duck!' Paula murmured, and followed Minnie to the kitchen. Sam, the odd-job man, stood there on the step, holding a plump young duck in his hands. He was peering at a card tied round its neck.

'Says it's fer yer Christmas dinner,' he said.

'Let me see,' Paula said, mystified. 'Oh, it's from Mr Lowther. How kind of him. What a beautiful bird!' She stroked the duck's glossy head, and it gave a soft little quack.

Rosalind came hurrying in. 'Mrs J's all right for the moment,' she said. 'Where is it? Who's it from?'

Paula pointed to the card. 'It's our Christmas dinner,' she said, and took the duck from Sam's gnarled hands. It gave another drowsy quack, and Paula murmured,

' "And God must be laughing still
At the sound that came out of its bill." '

'Not quite right,' Rosalind grinned, 'but near enough. It's a lovely plump one,' she remarked, feeling the duck's breast.

'I'll kill it fer yer,' Sam offered helpfully. 'Ought to be done now, and it'll be just bonzer fer Christmas Day.'

The two girls looked at each other, and then at Sam.

'Oh, we couldn't kill it,' Paula protested. 'Could we, Ross? I'd feel like a murderess, wouldn't you? No, Sam, thank you, we'll have something else for Christmas dinner.'

'Too true we will,' Rosalind agreed, chucking the duck under the bill. 'Why, it'd stick in my throat. Let's start a duckery,' she said to Paula, laughing. 'Minnie, have you got a nice big box, and—' The front door bell rang again, and Paula went to the kitchen door and looked out.

'The coach has stopped outside,' she said. 'Now I wonder—what's this? Looks like an accident. Come on, Ross,' and she almost ran out into the hall. They met the driver of the coach at the door. A passenger had hurried up and rung the bell.

'What is it?' Paula asked, standing aside for the driver to enter. He was carrying someone small in his arms. 'An accident?'

'No, Sister,' was the reply, 'just a kid taken ill. She suddenly crumpled up and sorter fainted. Happened just outside here, Sister, so I thought I'd better bring her in.'

'Yes, quite right. Along here,' Paula said. 'Lay her on the bed, will you? I'll see to her. You'll want to get back to the coach. Who is she, do you know?'

'No, I don't, miss. She was put on the coach at Hobart, and I did hear her say to another passenger that she was going to Dover for a holiday. This is her little case, but there's no name on it. If there's anyone waiting for her at the depot, I'll let them know where she is.'

'Thank you,' Paula said, and turned to look at the child on the bed. Her eyes were closed, and there was a pinched look about her small face.

Rosalind came in. 'Anything I can do?' she asked. 'What is it?'

Paula told her. 'Bring a bowl and some hot water, will you?' she said.

The child suddenly opened her eyes, shivered, and said in a weak voice, 'I think I'm going to be sick.' Rosalind reached quickly for the bowl on the washstand and gave it to Paula. They were just in time. Paula held the child's head till the attack was over.

'Better?' she enquired gently as the little girl fell back weakly on the pillows. 'Now, what has made you so sick? Did you eat something in the coach?'

'I can't—oh, it's coming again!'

The bell rang and Rosalind said hurriedly, 'That'll be Mrs Jenkins. I'd better go and see what she wants.'

Paula held the bowl for the child till the second attack was over, then she undressed her and got her into bed. She seemed scared and cried miserably. Paula comforted her as best she could, but she could get no information from the child as to what had caused the sickness. However, she's getting rid of it, Paula thought, which is the important thing.

'What is your name, dear?' she asked, but before the little girl could reply, another attack was threatening. 'Never mind,' Paula said after it was over, and she wiped the child's mouth. 'Just lie back now and rest.'

'My name's Hazel. Oh, am I going to die?' and the tears started again.

'Of course not.' Paula stroked back the damp fair hair from the child's brow. 'You'll soon be better. Now, I'm just going to take your temperature, then you must try to sleep.'

'How is she, Paula?' Rosalind asked from the door. 'Mrs Jenkins is doing nicely, by the way. Tomorrow morning, I'd say.'

'Good.' Paula walked to the door. 'This child's temp is very high,' she said in a low voice. 'Hundred and two. When Doctor comes I'll get him to look at her. You have phoned?' Rosalind nodded, and Paula went back to the child, who was now looking flushed and drowsy. Dr Renwick came in about ten minutes later.

'She's just dropped off to sleep,' Paula whispered to him. 'But she's been terribly sick—I think fruit. Temperature's a hundred and two.'

The doctor bent over the sleeping child. 'Umm,' he said presently. 'She seems peaceful enough now. Let her sleep it out, Paula. Then, when she wakes, give her an emetic just to be on the safe side. Good thing she's got it up. Let me know this evening how she is.' He studied the child's flushed face. 'Is she from the village? I don't seem to recognise her face, and I thought I knew most of the village kids.' Paula told him about the child's arrival, and he went on, remarking, 'No doubt the people to whom she was going will be up soon.'

Paula made certain the little girl was quite comfortable and still sleeping before she went out to see how Rosalind was getting on with her patient. She found her in the kitchen with Minnie and nursing the duck. Paula started to laugh.

'We're calling her Dilly,' Rosalind said. 'Mrs Jenkins is being lazy, so I've told her to walk up and down in her room.' She smoothed the duck's bill, and it ruffled its feathers complacently.

'Will you keep an eye on my little girl for a moment?'

Paula asked. 'I must wash and change my overall.' When she came from her room a few minutes later she saw Rosalind in the hall talking to a worried-looking middle-aged couple. She called to Paula and said,

'This lady and gentleman have come about the little girl.'

'Oh, yes,' Paula said, going to meet them, 'but please don't worry. She has been very sick, but is better now. I'm afraid you won't be able to see her,' she added, anticipating the question which she saw was coming. 'She's asleep, you see, and the doctor doesn't want her to be disturbed.' Paula went into a few details about the child's arrival after her collapse on the coach.

'Oh dear!' said the lady. 'I wonder if it was apples. It's spraying time. But I'm very relieved that she's getting better. She was coming to stay with us over Christmas. When do you think she will be well enough to come out, Sister?'

'The doctor is going to see her again this evening,' Paula said. 'Why not give us a ring about seven, and I'll probably be able to tell you then. May be tomorrow if her temperature is normal.'

'All right, Sister, we'll do that.' The couple walked to the door. 'Our name is Halliday. Will you give her our love, poor little Hazel.'

'I will. By the way,' Paula said, following them to the door, 'what is her other name?'

'Dane,' said the lady, just as Rosalind called from along the passage, 'Paula, can you come?'

'Goodbye,' Paula said hurriedly to the couple. 'I must go. Don't worry about Hazel, will you? She'll be all right tomorrow.'

'Could you give a hand?' Rosalind said a minute later. 'She's really getting on with things, aren't you, Mrs Jenkins?'

By eight o'clock that evening Master Colin Jenkins had announced his arrival in the world with a lusty roar; and Hazel was sitting up in bed looking much more cheerful. She admitted to Paula that during one of the coach's stops she had slipped into an orchard and picked an apple. 'But I had only one bite,' she said. 'I didn't like the taste.'

When Mrs Halliday telephoned that evening Paula was able to tell her that Hazel was better, and that she could call for her the following morning.

'Lovely!' Rosalind said later that evening as the two sat having supper together. 'The prospects for the party are decidedly hopeful. What are you going to wear, Paula?'

'My yellow, I think. Hello, Minnie, is that the mail?' as the latter entered with some papers and letters in her hand. 'It's late.' Paula took them from her, and opened first a square, official-looking envelope. 'Hmm,' she said presently, and passed it across to Rosalind. 'Our days here are numbered. The permanent Sister arrives within the next two weeks. I shall be quite sorry to go. How about you?' Paula looked up as there was no reply and was surprised to see the look of dismay on Rosalind's round face. 'I suppose it was to be expected,' she added uncertainly. 'After all, we are Tourist, you know.'

'Yes, I know, but I do like it here, don't you?'

'I love it,' Paula said. 'But anyway, Ross, we've got another couple of weeks, perhaps more; and we'll get the party in. No other cases are due yet, and Doc reminded me only yesterday that he and Susan are all set to come in on New Year's Eve.'

Luck was on the girls' side, and on New Year's Eve Mrs Jenkins and her baby were still the only patients. At seven o'clock Mr Lowther sent his car to bring the two girls to his house.

'Well, you certainly are a credit to the hospital,' Susan Renwick said admiringly. Her eyes travelled from Paula's cloudy dark hair and brilliant greenish eyes to Rosalind's blonde freshness. 'Enjoy yourselves,' she called after them as they went out to the car.

'I wish you were coming,' Paula said, turning round at the door.

'I don't,' was the reply. 'Frank and I hate parties.'

Paula laughed and waved to her. It was true, she knew. Susan Renwick, childless after ten years, was pathetically happy always to be back in the familiar atmosphere of mothers and babies. Paula caught Rosalind's eye, and suddenly the two were laughing joyously. They were young, they were good to look upon—and they were going to a party.

The house was of weatherboard, built in Colonial style—long and low, and with a flight of wide steps leading to a deep verandah which ran all round the house. There were festoons of fairy lights hanging from the eaves, and as the car swept up the wide gravel drive Paula saw that the tall red gum-trees which formed a natural setting for the house were also lit up with the brightly-coloured lights. The front of the verandah was hung with Chinese lanterns. It all looked very gay and festive. Several groups of people were gathered on the verandah and a maid was passing round with a tray of glasses.

Angus Lowther hurried forward as the car came to a standstill.

'Come along in, my dears,' he said, holding out both hands. 'I've been wondering all day if ye'd make it. So the bairns were kind to ye, eh?' He was wearing a white dinner jacket, and Paula thought how distinguished he looked with his boldly-featured face and steel-grey hair. He put an arm round the shoulders of each and drew them forward. 'Come and meet everyone,' he said, 'but first, drinks,' and he made a signal. 'Now this is Laura Stringer, and Robert.' He stopped before a couple in their mid-forties. There were smiles and handshakes, and a few commonplaces were exchanged; then on to a young man and a girl who, it appeared, were an engaged couple.

'And this is Philip Freeman,' Mr Lowther continued. 'He's been wanting to meet you. I gather he had a letter from his sister in London.'

'Why, of course!' Paula exclaimed. 'That nice girl at Tasmania House. We'd been meaning to contact you, hadn't we, Ross?' She smiled and held out a hand to a dark young man with merry blue eyes who was watching her with obvious admiration.

'Yes,' Rosalind agreed. He turned to her and held out his hand. 'But it isn't easy to get out together. This is a very special and lucky occasion.'

'Then we must have another one soon,' the young man said, turning again to Paula, who was sipping her cocktail. She was about to make some reply, but the words seemed to lose themselves. For over young Freeman's shoulder Paula had seen a face she knew. Christopher Deane was standing a few paces away, talking and laughing with a smart redheaded girl in black. Paula was surprised to see how young and boyish he could look. She did not know if he had seen her and wondered who the redhaired girl could be. Then she felt her elbow being taken and she was led forward again to meet more guests. Paula lost count of them, and despaired of remembering names; but suddenly she heard *his* voice beside her.

'Good evening, Paula,' Christopher said. 'How nice to see you again.' She looked up into the quiet grey eyes, and her breath seemed to catch in her throat. 'I want to thank you for looking after my daughter so well.'

CHAPTER EIGHT

'GOOD evening,' Paula said, trying to keep her voice calm, 'but—your daughter? I don't understand.'

He smiled down at her flushed face. 'Hazel,' he explained. 'She was taken ill on the coach. She—'

'Oh, that little girl,' Paula said. 'But—*your* daughter! Why, Mrs Halliday said her name was—' then she stopped in confusion. Of course, the Australian twang; but it had sounded like Dane. She saw that he was laughing at her and probably understood how she had come to mistake the name.

'Yes, Hazel is my daughter,' he continued, 'and you seem to have made a very good impression on her.'

Paula looked at him quickly and wondered if she had imagined an emphasis on the last word. 'I hope she has quite recovered,' she said very formally. She looked past him and saw that the girl in the black frock was talking to someone on her other side while Rosalind seemed to be enjoying a joke with Philip Freeman.

'You're looking very beautiful,' Christopher said, and Paula caught her breath as she met the glance of his grey eyes. There was a general stir throughout the room, and before Paula could think of a reply to his remark, the redheaded girl, whose name she knew now was Doreen, caught his arm and said,

'I think everyone's going in to dinner, Chris.' She looked coolly at Paula and took an even firmer grip of the arm she held.

'Ah, here you are, apple-blossom, come along.' It was Angus Lowther, and he put an arm round Paula's shoulders, and drew her towards the dining room. She saw that Rosalind was being escorted by Philip.

'Oh, how lovely!' Paula said at her first sight of the

room. There were large tubs of pink and blue
hydrangeas at either end, and along the length of the
dark polished table were slender silver vases containing
pink and white carnations and shadowy green maiden-
hair fern. The concealed lighting from the walls cast a
soft dim glow over the table. Paula saw that Rosalind
was sitting almost opposite her and next to Philip Freeman. Christopher and the redhead were down at the
other end. Mrs Stringer was at the opposite end of the
table to Angus and was obviously acting as hostess.

Angus Lowther was a good experienced host and kept
the ball of conversation rolling. Paula thought that
Rosalind looked rather put out, and wondered why. She
had been looking forward so to this party. Paula tried to
catch her eye, but was unsuccessful. The food was delicious, starting with cantaloup melon, on to scallops,
then roast duck. A soufflé *surprise* was followed by
coffee and liqueurs of several kinds. Paula was enjoying
every minute of it. There was a singing in her blood. She
had not expected to see Christopher—and he had said
she was beautiful. And though there was a nagging little
question in her mind as to the identity of the redhaired
girl, yet Paula felt that the evening had begun in a most
unexpected and exciting way.

After dinner was over a band appeared on the wide
verandah and dancing began. Paula was claimed at once
by Philip Freeman.

'I say, Paula,' he began at once, 'can't we make a date
to visit my place at Taroona? I asked your friend Rosalind, but she referred me to you.'

'We'd love to,' Paula replied, wondering where Christopher and his companion were. She could not see either
of them anywhere. 'But you see, it's only very seldom
that we can both get out together. Why not give me your
telephone number, and the very next time we're quiet at
the hospital we'll make a date?' As she spoke Paula saw
that he had guided her round the corner of the verandah
into semi-darkness.

'I'll do that,' Philip said, then as the music stopped,

'come and sit down over here while I write it down.' He led Paula to a half-hidden settee, and sat down very close to her. 'You're a lovely girl,' he said suddenly, and bent and kissed her cheek. Paula drew back sharply, but said nothing. After all, it was a party, she thought, and perhaps the drinks were having an effect on him. She herself felt starry-eyed and beautifully relaxed. She wondered again where Christopher was.

'There you are, Paula,' Philip said, holding out a card and catching her hand as she took it. Paula laughed and there was a light-hearted struggle between them. A voice behind them suddenly said, 'This is ours, I think.'

Her heart missed a beat as she looked up straight into the cool grey eyes of Christopher Deane. How long had he been there? she wondered. He put out a hand to her and Paula rose to her feet.

'Excuse me, Philip,' she murmured, and moved away beside Christopher. He led her by the arm in the direction of the steps.

'I thought you didn't dance,' Paula said rather breathlessly.

'We're not dancing,' he said, and led her down the steps and into the garden. 'There is something I want to ask you—just a matter of curiosity.' He drew her behind a mimosa bush, then stopped. He paused, looking down into her face, then said slowly, 'What did you mean—in Hobart that night—when you said you had something to explain?'

'Did I say that?' Paula asked; she had recovered her composure by now. 'I can't remember.' She giggled. The drinks she had had were making her feel reckless. 'It's a very long time ago, isn't it, and so much has happened in the meantime.' She looked at him, tall and handsome in the moonlight, and her heart beat so that she thought he must surely hear.

'Yes, I suppose so,' he said slowly. 'To someone as lovely as you something must be always happening.' Paula looked up and met the intent gaze of his eyes. 'I guess I'm a fool. Some of us never learn.' He laughed abruptly, not a nice laugh, she thought. 'And you—what are you, I wonder?'

She looked at him, puzzled at his tone. In her yellow frock, and with her cloudy black hair and brilliant hazel eyes, Paula was breathtakingly lovely. 'Yes, you're beautiful,' he said, and suddenly pulled her towards him. Paula gave a stifled gasp as his lips came down hard over hers. For a brief moment everything round her faded and she was conscious only of the almost delirious delight of his lips, and his arms around her. But just as suddenly he released her, so that Paula half staggered back.

'Come,' Christopher said in a hoarse, abrupt voice, 'I'll take you in again. I apologise.'

Paula looked in bewilderment at his half-averted face. She was still trembling from the most devastating uprush of emotion she had ever experienced. It was wonderful and shattering at the same time. Surely he had felt the same.

'But—but, Chris,' she half stammered, 'you—you needn't. You—'

'I know,' he interrupted almost violently. 'But forget it.' He reached out to take her arm, but Paula moved sharply back and stood facing him. Bright colour was in her cheeks, and her eyes flashed.

'Don't worry,' she said between her teeth. 'It's forgotten.' And turning on her heel she walked rapidly away. She thought she heard him call her name, but took no notice.

New Year's Day in Tasmania was as hot as August Bank Holiday in England. Paula looked out of her bedroom window to the bright glare of sea and sand. Roses bloomed in profusion in the hospital garden and Sam wandered about cutting off the heads of dead flowers. It was all so beautiful, Paula thought, and suddenly there was a lump in her throat. Oh, why had Christopher kissed her like that the night before, and then snubbed her so unmercifully? Before that had happened Paula had known that she liked him—very much; had recognised that she was strongly attracted to him. It had been a kind of undercurrent of excitement to her days—always there, but not forceful enough to disturb her unduly. Paula sighed, then dragged a comb irritably through her thick wavy hair. Christopher's kiss had awakened her to reality. She was afraid now that she was in love with him and that it was already too late to banish him from her thoughts. As for him, Paula was completely bewildered. He seemed to like yet despise her at the same time. Had he really read the worst possible meaning into Bob Shaw's words?

Paula took up her hairbrush, then banged it angrily down upon the dressing table. 'I'll forget him,' she muttered. 'I will. I'll put him right out of my mind. He's not going to be allowed to spoil my life. I've had my lesson!'

She finished dressing and went in to breakfast. Rosalind was already there in her place. The Renwicks had left earlier as he had his surgery to attend to.

'Well, the party's over,' Paula said, pouring herself a cup of coffee. 'Did you enjoy it?' She thought Rosalind looked pale.

'Yes,' Rosalind said in a rather flat voice, 'I thought it was very well got up.' Paula glanced at her across the table. Rosalind had not really answered her question. 'Quite a surprise to see Christopher there, wasn't it? Had he anything to say? I saw you talking to him just before dinner, and then he and his girl-friend seemed to disappear.'

So she didn't see us go into the garden together, Paula thought. I'm glad. I can't tell her about that. I can't tell anyone.

'No,' she said aloud. 'And I was very surprised to learn that Hazel—you remember, our little girl patient—was his daughter. He's down here to take her back after the holiday.'

'Oh!' Rosalind said. 'And who was the redhead?'

Paula shook her head and helped herself to toast. 'Haven't a clue,' she said.

The conversation languished after that, and Paula was left with the feeling that Rosalind was annoyed about something. She wondered if the latter had been attracted to Philip Freeman and had noticed his attentions to herself. Paula sighed wearily as she rose from the table. In spite of herself her thoughts slipped back to the evening before. After she had left Christopher in the garden she had run swiftly up the steps and made straight for the cloakroom. There she had stayed till she had regained her composure. When at last Paula had emerged a rousing and noisy Paul Jones was in progress, and it had been easy to slip into the circle of dancers. Christopher seemed to have gone, also the redhead.

Somewhat to her surprise Paula had enjoyed the rest of the evening. After the Paul Jones she had joined in The Gay Gordons with Angus for a partner. Then just before midnight a dish was brought in and handed round. A beautiful savoury smell came from it, and Angus announced that it was real Scots haggis, and that everyone must taste it. Paula found it delicious. More drinks were brought in, then suddenly a loud and prolonged pealing of the bell was heard. At the same time the clock in the room began to chime the hour of twelve, and on the last note Angus crossed the room to the darkened verandah and switched on all the lights. Paula stared. There on the top step was Christopher Deane. He was laughing as Angus took him by the arm and drew him forward.

'Give a welcome to the Dark Man,' he called to the guests. 'The first-footer of the New Year, come to bring this house good luck and prosperity for a twelvemonth. What gifts do you bring, Dark Man?'

Christopher laughed, and Paula saw that he was carrying a basket.

'The traditional ones,' he replied. 'A loaf of bread,' he dived into the basket with his hand, and brought out a small loaf. 'A lump of coal. Sorry, Angus, I could find only a log. Here it is,' he handed it to his host. 'And a purse of money. Well, a couple of coppers, anyway. Catch!'

There was general laughter after this, and a little later the party began to break up with the usual handshakes and slightly maudlin kissing. Paula had missed Rosalind while all this was going on, and it was not till she had bidden a very cold and formal goodnight to Christopher and his companion that Rosalind slipped into the room, followed by Philip Freeman. She was looking flushed and slightly defiant as she met Paula's eye. Finally, the band struck up 'Auld Lang Syne' and the party was over. Paula looked speculatively at Philip Freeman, and wondered about him and Rosalind. The two had spent most of the evening together, and Paula herself had deliberately sought out their host and stayed with him. Then Angus and Philip had seen the two girls back to the hospital.

Paula went towards the door just as the telephone in the hall jangled its summons. She went to answer it, but Minnie was already there.

'It's Miss Needham,' she said. 'She wants you.'

Paula picked up the receiver. 'That you, Paula?' came Miss Needham's voice. 'You got my letter about Sister Anderson arriving, did you?'

'Yes,' Paula replied. 'Any further news?'

'Yes. She'll be here on the tenth, and on the thirteenth I want one of you to go to Triabunna. It's a little one-Sister hospital just north of here. The Sister there, a Mrs Leslie, wants to take her holiday. Triabunna is on the coast. It's a little fishing and sailing place. It's only for a week, and it's a very quiet place. Anyway, Paula, let me know soon which one of you will be going. How are you both? Good. Well, a happy New Year to you. Goodbye.'

'That was Miss Needham,' Paula said to Rosalind, who was waiting nearby, and told her what she had said. 'Well, who'd like to go to Triabunna? She left it to us.'

'All right—who?' Rosalind asked in an uninterested voice.

Paula looked at her, puzzled and slightly worried at her tone. 'I don't mind going,' she said, 'but if you'd like a change then I'm quite happy to stay put.'

Rosalind said nothing. She strolled to the door and looked out. 'Well, if you really don't mind either way,' she said at last, 'I'd rather stay here.'

'O.K. That's settled, then. I might as well ring Miss Needham at once.' She waited a moment, then as Rosalind did not reply, Paula picked up the receiver.

Just before midday a young workman was brought in by a group of his friends. They had been felling trees a little way up the road, and he had brought the axe down on to his foot. Rosalind was with Mrs Jenkins, so Paula admitted the young man. He grinned at her sheepishly though obviously in great pain, and muttered, 'Sorry, Sister. Fair cow this, ain't it?'

When she had disengaged the gashed foot and sock from his foot, Paula almost gasped. The wound was a full inch deep, across the instep and part of the great toe. She cleaned it up and fixed an emergency first-aid dressing, then went quickly to the telephone. Dr Renwick would be in at six, but Paula felt that this could not wait till then. Rosalind came into the hall just as she put the receiver down.

'What is it, Paula?' she asked.

'I've been trying to get Dr Renwick,' was the reply, and she told Rosalind about the latest patient. 'I'm not too happy about him,' she added. 'I'm going back now to make him as comfortable as I can, but will you try one or two numbers where Doctor might be, Ross? Try the post office, and—and Angus Lowther, perhaps. He calls there sometimes.'

'Yes, all right. I'll do what I can. Mrs Jenkins and the baby are all right till next feed time.'

Half an hour later Rosalind went to find Paula.

'No luck, I'm afraid,' she told her. 'Susan Renwick doesn't know, and he hasn't been to the Lowther house, and—'

'Never mind, Ross,' Paula interrupted. She had just

come out of the patient's room. 'I've done what I can.
I've fixed a splint on the toe, with a tight bandage.
He's had a T.T. injection and, so far, says he feels all
right.'

'What about penicillin?' Rosalind asked.

'Yes, I've started that. A million units, I think, don't
you? Oh, if you'd seen it, Ross, when he came in. I
sutured the wound, of course. It had to be done; he was
losing such a lot of blood.'

Rosalind looked at Paula's face. 'Go and get some
dinner,' she suggested. 'Minnie has kept it hot. I'll keep
an eye on him.'

At five Susan Renwick rang to say that the doctor was
on his way to the hospital, and he arrived almost at once.
Paula, looking flushed and tired, took him at once to the
bedside of her patient. After she had removed the dressing, he carefully examined the wound, asked a few brief
questions, then beckoned Paula outside.

'Sister, that's a damn fine job you've done in there,' he
said, smiling and patting her on the shoulder. 'In fact,'
he grinned into her tired face, 'a real beaut. Couldn't
have done it better myself! Now you go and get Minnie
to make you a good strong cup of tea. He'll be all right
now.'

Paula's patient made good progress during the next
few days. Then a child suffering from mild sunstroke was
brought in by her mother and recovered in due course.
Life dropped into its usual quiet summer routine, and
except for the odd casualty and the young man with the
foot wound, by the time that Sister Anderson was due to
arrive the little hospital was practically empty.

'It's always like this during the summer months,' Dr
Renwick said in reply to a remark made by Rosalind.
'Winter's the busy time, just as it is at home. Now listen,
girls—' they were all sitting over the ever-present pot of
tea as he spoke. 'With the new Sister arriving today, and
Paula not going to Triabunna till the thirteenth, make
the most of the next couple of days, my children. Get out
somewhere together. You don't often get the chance.

Ah, this sounds like the coach. Let's go and meet Sister Anderson.'

The new Sister-in-charge turned out to be a pleasant, buxom young woman in the late twenties. She had already spent three years in the Australian bush, and was a great friend of Miss Needham. After tea she briskly insisted on taking over from Paula, then after that went with the two girls to meet the patients, Mrs Jenkins, who was leaving that same evening, and Tom, the young man with the cut foot, who was going out the next day. In the kitchen they found Mrs Aust, who had supposedly brought Sandra up to be weighed, but was really there for a gossip with Minnie.

'Oh, and this is Dilly,' Paula said, laughing, as the fat duck waddled in at the back door. 'She was our Christmas dinner, but we just hadn't the heart.'

'I should just think not,' Betty Anderson said, 'And as far as I'm concerned she's safe over next Christmas too.'

'Ross,' Paula said that evening just before bedtime, 'what about making a date with Philip Freeman, to visit his home at—what was the name of the place? Oh, Taroona, that was it. He gave me his telephone number.' She looked quickly at Rosalind, wondering if the last sentence had been a mistake. But the latter seemed quite unconcerned. She had been more like her old self lately, Paula thought. 'It's a grand opportunity,' she continued hastily. 'Shall we telephone him and suggest the twelfth? I think Sister Anderson would be quite pleased to be on her own with Dr Renwick for a day.'

'Yes, I'm all for it,' Rosalind replied, quite in her old cheery manner. 'Let's ring now. It's not awfully late.'

Philip Freeman was delighted when Paula made her suggestion for the visit, and arrangements were quickly made. Quite early on the morning of the twelfth he called for the two girls in an old Ford convertible, and after a run of about three hours they arrived at a big, rather ugly red-brick house set in its own grounds. The girls were given a cordial welcome by Philip's parents and his young brother William. After dinner was over Philip said to his father, 'What about taking the girls to Cygnet?'

'Cygnet! Is that a place?' Rosalind asked. 'I always thought it was a young swan.'

Philip laughed. 'This happens to be a place,' he said. 'And our apple-orchards are there. You'll have to visit them again in March when we have the Apple Festival. How about one of you having a shot at being elected Apple Queen?'

The two girls laughed, and Mr Freeman senior remarked gallantly, 'A couple o' bonzer kids like you ought to stand a good chance.' Everyone burst out laughing, then Philip said, grinning,

'Too right they should, Dad. Come on, girls, let's go.'

'Gosh, what a lot!' Rosalind exclaimed about an hour later as she and Paula were led up one long avenue of apple-trees and down another. 'Who looks after the estate?'

'I look after this one,' Philip said, then, at her look of surprise, 'yes, really. Dad has given me the day off to look after you both. Now there—' he pointed, 'are the packing sheds. You see they are all numbered. Different varieties and grades go into each. They're stored here till it's time to take them into Hobart for export.'

After tea at Philip's home, a friend of his arrived in a long, sleek, American car. He was a merry-looking individual with a roving eye, and was introduced as Tim Halloran. The girls soon gathered that he was one of Hobart's leading business men.

'We thought you'd like to have a trip up our mountain,' Philip said, looking at Rosalind.

'Mount Wellington?' she exclaimed, blue eyes opening wide with delight. 'Why, that's what we've always wanted to do, isn't it, Paula?'

'There's nothing I'd like to do better.' Paula's hazel eyes also were sparkling. Not only was she delighted at the prospect of the trip, but Philip seemed to have definitely transferred his interest to Rosalind, while she apparently was to be partnered off with Tim. The latter looked to be an amusing person, so the arrangement suited Paula very well.

'Good,' Philip said. 'Then let's get going.' Goodbyes were said to Philip's parents with promises to visit again, and then the four young people set off. The powerful car devoured the miles, streaking through a place called Ferntree and then beginning the ascent of the mountain. They could see the road above them snaking in and out between the wooded slopes, going higher and higher till it was lost to view.

'Oh, what a gorgeous view!' Paula exclaimed as the car rounded a bend and crawled cautiously forward.

'Wait till you see the view from the top,' Tim said, watching her excited face. 'This is nothing,' he added, manoeuvring the car round a particularly sharp and frightening bend. Paula gave one look, then stared straight ahead, trying not to look worried.

The sun was just setting as they reached the look-out at the top of Mount Wellington. It was merely a concrete platform with stout railings running its entire length.

'Well, girls, here we are,' Philip said, helping Rosalind out of the car. 'Come along,' and he took an arm of each and led them to the platform. 'What do you think of it?' He waved an arm at the panoramic view that was spread out miles and miles below them.

There was complete silence for a moment, then Paula let out a long "oh" of delight.

'It's wonderful,' she said softly, and Rosalind beside her murmured,

'Oh, Philip, what a marvellous, marvellous view! I could go on looking at it for ever.'

'So could I,' Paula breathed. 'Just look at those colours!'

The mountain slopes were clothed completely in every shade of green. The valley, bathed in the rays of the setting sun, was pale green and gold. Silver ribbons of rivers wound their way between carpets of tender green, and dotted about at intervals were the clustered roofs and spires of villages. The sky was streaked with swathes of pink, green and gold; and forming a frame for all this beauty was the curving, white-edged blue of the sea.

'Yes, it's a wonderful view, best in the island,' Tim agreed rather prosaically, then, seeing Paula give a little shiver, 'Cold?' She shook her head, but Philip took Rosalind by the arm.

'Come on,' he said. 'We'll go and eat. The hotel's just a little way down the road. You probably noticed it as we passed.' He turned to speak to Tim. 'We've got to get these girls back in good time. It is tomorrow you leave for Triabunna, Paula, isn't it?'

'I'd love to spend a whole day here,' Rosalind said, as they all climbed into the car again.

'When you do just let me know, won't you?' Paula heard Philip reply from the back seat.

'So you're off to Triabunna, eh?' Tim said presently as the car drew up before the hotel. Paula nodded. She was looking with lively interest at the entrance to Springs Hotel, Mount Wellington. It looked much more like an English country club than a hotel, Paula thought. It was white, half-timbered, and had several tall gables. It stood well back from the road in a beautiful natural setting of pine-trees. A steep path, protected by a rustic railing, led up to the wide front porch.

'Well, here we are,' Tim said, leading the way into the dining room. A waiter hurried up and led the party to a table by a window.

'Oh, goody, scallops!' Paula said, picking up the menu. 'And am I hungry!' She looked round and saw that the room was almost full. There was a pleasant hum of voices, and from somewhere unseen an orchestra played.

The meal progressed comfortably and happily to the coffee and cigarette stage. Philip laughed and joked with Rosalind while Tim kept up a pleasantly casual conversation with Paula. But presently he looked at his watch and remarked, 'I think we should make a move.

We've got quite a distance to cover. Come on, Phil,' he added, turning to the other man, 'finish your smoke, and then—away.'

'Oh, so soon!' Rosalind said, then, sighing, 'Well, I suppose we must.' Tim put a hand on Paula's and drew her to her feet, and Philip stubbed out his cigarette, and with an arm round Rosalind's waist, started to follow the other two to the door. They threaded their way between tables, and it was not till they were nearly there that Paula saw Christopher. He and the redhaired girl, Doreen, were sitting at a table for two. Paula felt the blood surge to her face as the memory of their last meeting came before her. Ever since that night in the garden of Angus's house she had striven to put the thought of Christopher's kiss from her mind, for she felt that, coupled with the words he had spoken, it was almost an insult. But it had been a difficult task, and, in spite of herself, her heart now beat with painful intensity as she met the sudden glance of his eyes.

'Enjoyed the evening, Paula?' she heard Tim say, and at the same moment another voice spoke.

'Hello, Paula,' he said. 'You do get around, don't you? Hello, Rosalind.' Paula turned her head slowly and looked at him. He was standing now and smiling—all except his eyes. They were looking straight into hers, with a peculiar look in them—a questioning look, she thought. Paula hesitated for a second, then she thought again of their last meeting, and her face hardened.

Christopher took a step forward, but at the same moment Philip, who was behind Rosalind, said,

'Oh, hello, didn't we meet at the Lowther New Year's Eve party?'

Christopher turned as with an effort, looked at Philip, smiled suddenly and said, 'Why—er—yes, of course we did. How are you?' He looked again at Paula's expressionless face, and added, 'Won't you—join us for a drink?'

Philip hesitated, glancing appreciatively at the redhead, but Paula turned to Tim and said in a clear voice,

'We can't really spare the time, Tim, can we?' She almost turned her back on Christopher, who bowed, muttered something that Paula failed to catch, and resumed his seat beside his companion. Tim and Paula moved on, followed by Philip and Rosalind.

'Bit offhand, Paula, weren't you?' Philip observed mildly. 'I thought the girl friend looked quite a dish.'

'What an outrageous flirt you are, Philip!' Rosalind said, laughing, but Paula thought she sounded rather annoyed. 'Who is the woman anyway?'

Tim shrugged his shoulders. 'I've never seen her before,' he said, 'but, as Phil says, she's quite a looker. I did hear, by the way, that Deane is off to the mainland—for good. Don't know if it's true.'

'She was at the Lowther party, too,' Philip said, leading the way to the car. 'She was with Deane then. Don't you remember her, Rosalind?'

'Oh, yes, but she didn't look as if she wanted to know us tonight. In fact, she looked distinctly annoyed at our friend Christopher's suggestion re joining them for a drink. But who is she, anyway?'

Paula strained her ears for Philip's reply. Was this girl the reason for Christopher's departure for the mainland—that was, if it were true? She hurried after Philip and Rosalind.

'Well, her name's Doreen,' she heard him say. 'Pretty name, don't you think?' he added teasingly. 'She's from the mainland, I believe.' Paula's heart plunged heavily. 'And I hear that the said Mr Deane is thinking of having a second go in the matrimonial stakes.'

Paula walked on after Rosalind without noticing where she was going. Her heart had seemed to stop beating, then start again with sickening thuds. Was it true?

Rosalind turned and looked at Paula. 'D'you mean those two are engaged?' she asked.

CHAPTER NINE

EARLY the next morning Paula left for Triabunna. And
as she climbed up into the coach she thought with relief
that she would be glad to get away on her own for a few
days. She had tried hard not to dwell upon the previous
night's meeting with Christopher. It had been such a
lovely day, and she and Rosalind had enjoyed it all so
much—the meeting with Philip's jolly family; the visit to
the Freeman apple orchards, the exhilarating drive up
the mountain, and the glorious view at the top, and then,
last of all, the delicious meal at the picturesque Springs
Hotel. It had been such a happy day—till the sudden
meeting with Christopher and his companion. Why does
he have to keep spoiling my happiness? Paula thought
resentfully. Why can't he leave me alone?

And then came another thought, a thought which had
been at the back of her mind ever since last night. Was it
true what Philip had said—about Christopher's coming
marriage? In the bustle of departure he had not replied
to Rosalind's last question, and she had not pressed it.
Well, it's no business of mine, Paula thought now, and
with a determined effort she bent her mind to what lay
ahead of her. At the moment of departure Rosalind had
whispered,

'Gosh, I shall miss you.' Paula had given her a quick,
grateful smile, thinking with a sense of relief that Rosalind was her old cheery self again.

'I'll give you a tinkle when I get there,' she had
replied, 'and it's only for a week, you know.' And now,
as the coach set off, she turned and waved to Rosalind,
then set herself determinedly to enjoy the journey. It
was not really difficult, for, with her usual lively interest
in the events of the moment, Paula found that she was
able to banish her earlier unhappy musings, and enjoy
what was going on around her.

The first part of the journey took her through the now-familiar apple- and pear-orchards. This soon gave way to fields and cultivated lands with farms adjoining. The coach passed through several small villages, and Paula was much intrigued by the novel manner in which mail between the villages was delivered and collected. At intervals all along the route, and usually outside a fair-sized farm, a pole was fixed at right angles to a tall tree. It stuck out over the road, and hanging on a hook at the end of the pole was a sack. As the driver of the coach approached the pole, he slowed down, threw a sack of mail on to the side of the road, then deftly unhooked the sack from the pole, and drew it in through the window. Paula was amazed at the neat way it was done.

'Practice makes perfect,' the driver said to her with a friendly grin. 'It helps out the post office, you see.' The road now began to follow the course of a river. 'This is the Prosser,' he continued, nodding his head towards the river. 'We'll be passing through Oxford next. See that old road over there, across the river,' he nodded his head again. Paula looked, and saw between the pine-trees on the opposite side of the gleaming river a barely discernible cobbled track. It stretched as far as she could see, but did not seem to be in use. 'That road was built by the convicts nearly a hundred years ago, and cost a good few lives, too, poor devils.'

It was nearly midday when the coach arrived at Triabunna, a picture-postcard village on the shores of Spring Bay. Paula stepped down and looked around her with pleased interest. The sea was blue, the sun shone warmly down, and the bright sails of yachts sped across the little bay.

'Ah, there you are,' said a voice behind her. 'I'm sure you are Miss Bruce, and I'm Mrs Leslie.' Paula turned and saw a pleasant-faced woman in the late forties. She had just stepped out of a small Morris Minor car, and was holding out a welcoming hand.

Paula smiled as she went to meet her. 'Yes, I'm Paula Bruce,' she said. 'Thank you for coming to meet me.'

'Hop in,' said Mrs Leslie, opening the car door. 'I was down this way shopping, so I thought I'd wait and meet the coach. Did you have a good journey?' She started the engine and the little car shot up the road.

'It was most interesting,' Paula replied. 'I'm new enough to Tasmania to see something different almost everywhere I go. Your hospital is quite small, I believe.'

Sister Leslie laughed as the car turned in at a wide gate. 'That's right,' she said. 'And here it is.' Paula looked and smiled. She had thought the Dover hospital small, but this was hardly more than a cottage. 'But it suits me fine,' Mrs Leslie continued. 'I'm a widow with a daughter at boarding school, and this is home for us both. I'm thankful for it. Come along in. I'll put the car away presently.' Paula followed her into a tiny living room. 'Dinner is ready, and then I'll show you over the place. But first you'll want to go to your room, of course. Along here.'

It was a pleasant room, Paula found, with a wide window looking out on to the bay. She had a quick wash, tidied her hair, then went back to the living room where she found that dinner had just been brought in.

'This is Mrs Swain, our cook,' Sister Leslie said, and Paula smiled and shook hands with the quiet-looking woman who was just turning to go back to the kitchen. 'She's a treasure,' Mrs Leslie added as the door closed behind her.

'How many patients have you?' Paula asked, picking up her soup spoon.

'Only one at present, and she'll be out soon.'

'Maternity?' Paula looked round the room as she spoke. As well as a living room it seemed to be the office, for at one end was a desk, a small filing cabinet, and a telephone.

'No. Glandular fever,' was the reply. 'There's no special treatment, of course, just rest, and quiet, and watch the temperature. It's been steady for the last two days. I've got her case sheet and chart for you to look at on the desk,' she motioned to the end of the room, 'and

I'll take you to see her as soon as you've settled in. By the way, we only take women and children here. It's a one-Sister hospital, you see; it's a rule. Most of our cases are maternity and there's no one due for a couple of weeks, so you should have a quiet time.'

Paula sighed inwardly. She had been hoping for just the reverse, to keep her thoughts away from other matters. 'Now, about your time off,' Sister Leslie went on, 'it has to be carefully organised in a one-Sister hospital. You must work it out so that you are on call, and can be contacted easily. I've got a list of telephone numbers which I keep over my desk. There's the post office first, then the shops, the Spring Hotel, the library, and of course, the visiting doctor. Mrs Swain knows exactly what to do if there's a message, or a patient arrives while I'm out. She just goes through the numbers, starting with the post office.'

Paula nodded thoughtfully. 'I see,' she said, 'but isn't it a bit chancy?'

Sister Leslie smiled. 'Not really,' she replied. 'You see, Triabunna is such a tiny place that almost anywhere is within minutes of getting back here. Maternity cases are always told to come in early and to give us good warning. No, you have nothing to worry about.'

'What about an emergency if it happens to be a man?' Paula then asked.

Mrs Leslie poured coffee and passed a cup across the table. 'Well, that's different, of course,' she said. 'Only last week I had an accident case brought in—a hand wound. It needed four stitches, and I kept him in all night because of shock. It's really a matter of common sense. Well now, let me see. Yes, the visiting doctor, Strang's his name, comes here twice a week. He conducts his surgery, then visits our beds. He's due to-morrow, comes along about ten. Now, would you like to meet your patient?' she smiled at Paula. 'Sorry there aren't more.'

The next morning Sister Leslie departed in the Morris for her holiday. 'I don't really want to go,' she confided to Paula, 'but it's Founder's Week at the school, and Betty, my daughter, would be disappointed if I didn't go along, so—' she shrugged her shoulders and climbed into the little car.

Paula waved her goodbye, then hurried in to make ready for Dr Strang's surgery. She heard his car arrive just as she had finished, and went to the front door to meet him.

'Ah, Sister Bruce, isn't it?' he said, smiling at Paula, but soon hurried off to his surgery, which was a room in the hospital. Paula followed him and saw that everything was ready. One patient only turned up, an old man with a gumboil. After he had gone, Paula said,

'Would you like a cup of tea before seeing the patient here, Doctor?' He was a thin, rather frail-looking man, and she thought he looked tired.

'Thank you, Sister,' he said gratefully, and Paula hurried off to see Mrs Swain.

'How long are you here for?' he asked when she had returned with the tray. 'This is a quiet little place, especially in the summer months. I visit Swansea tomorrow. Have you been there?'

Paula poured the tea and passed it to him. 'No,' she said. 'So far I've only been to Dover, but then I haven't been in the Tourist service very long.'

He put down his cup and stood up. 'Well, Sister, shall we visit the patient?' he asked. 'Thanks for the tea, by the way.'

Mrs Donaldson, the patient with glandular fever, was a quiet woman who spent most of her time reading. 'There's such a lot to do at home, Sister,' she said to Paula after the doctor had gone, 'and this is such a heaven-sent opportunity to do some reading. I'm going to make the most of it.'

Paula went back to the living room and opened the list of bookings. She noted that the maternity case due in two weeks was a first baby. Might be early, Paula thought hopefully. The unexpected often happens with a first.

On the second day of her stay in Triabunna Paula managed to keep quite busy. Dr Strang had told her that he would be coming out again in two days' time, earlier if she wanted him, so Paula checked up on everything in case of emergency. She made quite certain that the sterilising drums, the sets of instruments, bowls and kidney dishes, gas and air apparatus and gowns and masks were all to hand. Mrs Swain was a great help as she had been there for a number of years and knew where everything was. But by supper-time Paula was getting very bored indeed. She was also rather depressed, as she was finding it increasingly difficult to keep her thoughts away from Christopher Deane. She had found the little library in the village and had picked out an interesting-looking book called *Flynn of the Inland* which kept her quite absorbed for a time.

But by the fourth day, when Mrs Donaldson left the hospital, Paula was beginning to long to return to Dover. Her only patient that day was a small boy who was brought in, howling loudly, by his bigger brother.

'What's the matter with him?' Paula asked of the bigger lad.

' 'E's eat some poison berries,' was the reply. 'Got a pain in 'is belly, fair cow 'e says it is, Sister.'

Paula bent over the sufferer. 'Tell me where the pain is,' she said, and sat him on a chair. 'Have you any of these berries with you?'

'I got one,' said the older boy, and produced a hip berry from his pocket.

'Oh, that's not poisonous,' Paula told him, 'but they'll give you a tummy-ache if you eat them raw,' she added. 'Now,' turning to the little chap, 'stop crying and I'll give you something nice that will soon fix it.'

The older boy watched with interest as Paula mixed a good-sized dose of milk of magnesia.

'There you are,' she said. 'Drink that, dear, and I've got a nice big chocolate for you when you've finished it.'

'Can I 'ave a dose, Sister?' asked big brother.

Paula ruffled his hair. 'You cannot,' she said, smiling.

'But here's a chocolate just the same. Take your little brother straight home now.'

After tea on the following day Paula suddenly felt that she must have some exercise. 'I'm going to walk across the fields to the village,' she said to Mrs Swain. 'I'll call in at the hotel, so if you want me you'll know where to telephone me.'

It was a lovely late afternoon when Paula set off. Spring Bay glittered blue and gold under the rays of the setting sun. Yachts with brilliantly-shining sails skimmed across its surface, and from the nearby hedges the hot sweet scent of honeysuckle drifted across to Paula as she strolled leisurely along the narrow footpath. Gradually the beauty and serenity of the scene had its effect on her and she found her restlessness subsiding and a peaceful sort of optimism taking its place.

Within ten minutes of starting Paula had reached the opposite side of the field and had stepped out on to the road. Opposite was the post office, and she called in on the offchance of there being some mail for the hospital, but found there was none. Turning to the right, Paula continued her walk, past the three or four cottages on the main road, then the half-dozen shops, till she reached Spring Bay Hotel. It was patronised almost exclusively by sailing and fishing enthusiasts, but at this time in the late afternoon was almost empty. Paula went in, thinking she would have a cold drink before making the return journey, but to her surprise the girl at the reception desk called to her.

'It is Sister Bruce, isn't it?' she asked, and as Paula murmured assent and came over, she continued, 'Mrs Swain from the hospital rang a few minutes ago. She said there was someone wanted to see you, but there was no hurry.'

Paula looked puzzled. 'Thank you,' she said to the girl, and turned again to the door. What could have happened during the short time she had been away, and why was there no hurry? It might be the baby case, of course, and Mrs Swain was almost certain to be very knowledgeable about such things, but Paula decided to go straight back just in case.

She crossed the field by the same path, walked through the small garden, and went straight into the dim, cool living room. There was not a sound, and Paula was just turning to go into the kitchen when a tall figure rose from the couch. For one brief bewildering moment she thought—and then her heart regained its normal position, for she had recognised the man who was standing there with outstretched hands. It was Angus Lowther.

'Hello, Paula,' he said, coming forward and placing both hands on her shoulders. 'Surprised to see me?'

'Well, of course,' she answered, trying to hide her irrational disappointment. 'When did you arrive, and what are you doing here, Angus? Oh, was that what Mrs Swain's cryptic message was about?'

He laughed. 'I imagine it was. I didn't want you to be worried, but I couldn't stay long, d'you see?'

'Oh, what a pity,' Paula said. 'Can't you even stay for a drink?'

'Sorry, but I'm meeting some other chaps for fishing in about ten minutes.'

'Well, sit down for a minute,' Paula said. 'It was nice of you to look me up. How did you know I was here?' She went to the couch.

'I met Chris Deane in Hobart yesterday,' he said unexpectedly as he sat down beside her. 'He happened to mention it.'

'Sure you won't have a drink?' Paula asked. She told herself she was no longer interested in Christopher Deane.

'No, thanks. I really came to invite you to go sailing,' he said hopefully.

'Oh, I'd have loved it,' Paula said regretfully. 'And it's very kind of you to think of it, Angus. But it's quite impossible, I'm afraid. This is a one-Sister hospital, you see. Didn't you know?'

He shook his head and looked disappointed. 'Well,

that's bad luck—for me,' he said. 'I'd been looking forward to showing you my boat.' He grinned like a schoolboy. 'She's a Cadet. I built her myself. Got the plans from London, and I've been sailing her now for a couple of years. Goes like a bird. Know anything about sailing, Paula?' Pride and enthusiasm glowed in his face and sounded in his voice as he spoke.

'A little,' she said. 'I crewed for—a friend, several times last year, on the Solent.' It was Bob Shaw she had sailed with, of course, and Paula sighed half regretfully as she recalled the fun they had had.

'Did you now?' Angus regarded her with interest. 'The Solent, eh? Are you sure you can't make it, Paula, just for an hour?' Then, as she shook her head regretfully, he rose to his feet. 'Well, then, how about dinner with me tonight—at the hotel?' Paula hesitated. She could be contacted easily at the hotel, and it would be fun to go out for a gay, carefree evening with Angus, he was such good company.

'Come on,' he urged, watching her face.

Paula laughed. 'How would it be if I gave you a ring?' she suggested. 'At about seven, perhaps.'

'That would be fine,' Angus agreed. 'That's a date, then—I hope. Till then—' and with an affectionate pat of her cheek, he took his leave.

Nice kind man, Paula thought, as she wandered through to the kitchen in search of a cup of tea.

'Kettle's boiling,' said Mrs Swain. 'I thought perhaps your friend would like a cup.'

'No, he couldn't stay,' Paula replied, and as she spoke, footsteps sounded in the living room. 'Now, who can—' she was beginning, when Sister Leslie's face appeared round the door. She burst out laughing at Paula's surprised look.

'I know what you're going to say,' she remarked coming towards her. 'That I'm not due back for another two days. Got a cup of tea, Mrs Swain? As a matter of fact I got so bored that I decided to come back early. My girl is at school at Launceston, you know,' she stirred her tea.

'It was her I went to see, but after five days I began to think of all kinds of things I wanted to do here. It's my home, you see. You don't mind, do you?' She looked at Paula.

'Of course not,' Paula laughed, 'but there's nothing doing here. In fact, I feel a complete fraud. Come and tell me about Launceston. Thanks, Mrs Swain.' She put her cup down and followed Sister Leslie into the living room. And it was not till well past seven that Paula remembered the tentative dinner date, and hurried to the telephone. But Mr Lowther had not yet returned, the receptionist at the hotel told her. Would the lady like to leave a message?

'Just tell him that Miss Bruce called,' Paula said, and as she hung up a sudden thought struck her. She could go sailing with Angus after all—that was, if Mrs Leslie did not mind.

Angus rang back after nine. He was full of apologies; the fishing party had only just returned. When Paula told him of Sister Leslie's unexpected return, he almost roared down the phone,

'Then you can come sailing with me after all? I'll call for you at nine tomorrow morning.'

'But, Angus,' Paula protested, laughing, 'I'll have to ask her if she minds.'

'Then you ask her right away, my lass. I suppose you've had dinner? Sorry about that, Paula. Now look, you run away and ask Mrs Leslie, and I'll be around at nine tomorrow.'

When Paula told her of the invitation to go sailing, Mrs Leslie urged her at once to accept. 'Of course,' she said with enthusiasm. 'No reason at all why you shouldn't. You go and enjoy yourself. It's too good an opportunity to miss—and you're only young once, you know.' She smiled archly at Paula, evidently scenting a romance. The latter thanked her, and so it was arranged.

The morning sun shone down on Paula's dark head as she stepped aboard the trim little Cadet. On the bows, in gold letters, was her name, *Adventure*. Angus, her

skipper, looked approvingly at his companion. Paula
was wearing red jeans and a yellow sun-top. Her grey-
green eyes sparkled with anticipation, and the wide red
mouth turned up at the corners as she met his smiling
glance. She thought suddenly that he looked very handsome in his white shorts and shirt, and wondered all at
once why he had never married.

'You sit over there, Paula, and take the tiller,' Angus
called, busy at the halyards. 'You're going to crew for
me today, did you know?'

Paula laughed up at him. 'Am I really?' she said.
'Well, I'm a good strong swimmer.'

'That's not a very tactful remark.' He grinned at her
across his shoulder. 'Looks as if you expect to be tipped
into the drink.'

'Oh, no,' she protested, laughing. 'Not expect, I'm
just prepared, that's all.'

'Well, off we go.' He came and sat beside her as the
wind filled the sails and the boat slid smoothly off. Paula
looked about her, at the blue sparkling sea, the splashes
of vivid colour from the sails of other yachts, at the
slowly-receding jetty and the hotel on the shore. And
then she turned and smiled delightedly into Angus's
brown face.

'Oh, this is marvellous,' she said, laughing for the
sheer joy of living. Her black hair streamed out behind
her, showing up in contrast the creamy whiteness of her
shoulders and arms, and her teeth gleamed between her
red lips as she turned to Angus. 'Isn't it beautiful?'

'It certainly is,' he replied softly, but his eyes were on
Paula's face and not the view. 'You make me feel young
again, Paula. Just to look at you now makes the whole
world seem new.'

She laughed and looked away from him. 'Angus, why
have you never married?' Paula asked, after a pause.
'You're so—nice. I can't think how you've escaped
it.'

He grinned, then said slowly, 'Well, there are reasons.
The old ticker, for one.'

'Oh, but that's all right so long as you're careful,' Paula protested. 'It isn't as if it's—'

'No,' he interrupted, then shrugged his shoulders. 'No—well, I guess it will last out, but—' he hesitated, seemed about to say more then evidently changed his mind. 'I've brought a picnic lunch, Paula. Cold chicken, salad and fruit. Does it appeal to you?'

'Sounds lovely. Angus, may I have a go at sailing? I've done just a little.'

'Sure. Why not,' he said at once. 'Change places with me. Now, I expect you know all about sails. This is a Bermudan mainsail. These ropes are the halyards and we're sailing now on the port tack. I'll take the tiller. Right?' He watched for a moment. 'Let her out a little. That's it. Look, I'm now going to push the tiller a little to starboard and you'll see the helm will swing to port. Now, haul on the mainsheet—not too much—that's about right. You're doing fine.' There was a short contented silence between them. Angus was watching Paula's slim figure and upraised arm and thinking what a lovely picture she made. 'Anything like this on the Solent?' he asked.

'Well, it was a bigger craft,' Paula replied, letting the rope slide through her hands and watching the bellying sail. 'A Firefly, I think it was.' She laughed. 'I was only allowed to crew on that.'

'We'll make the island for lunch,' Angus said after a further silence. 'Over there,' he pointed. 'Better let me take over now, Paula. You take the tiller, and be ready to pick up a mooring when we get there.'

'Is it really lunch-time?' Paula exclaimed in surprise as she changed places with Angus. 'Why, the morning has just flown. I must be back before tea,' she added. 'Just in case my patients come in.'

'We'll be in in good time,' he promised. 'Ready? See that iron ring on the bit that sticks out? Now—good girl, just made it. Neatly done, my dear. Now for some refreshment—and I, for one, am ready for it.'

The wind was freshening as, refreshed and fed, the

skipper and crew of *Adventure* started off once more.

'Can I have another go?' Paula asked, looking eagerly at Angus, but after a short pause he shook his head.

'Look over there,' he said, pointing to the horizon. Clouds piling up. Looks like a spot of bad weather. Might not come to anything, but I think we'd better get back. Wind's beginning to rise, too. You sit over there.' Paula looked over the side of the boat. She noticed with a pleasant little tingling of excitement that brisk, white-topped wavelets were slapping at their sides and the wind seemed to be blowing all ways at once.

'Paula,' Angus was forward and busy with the strain-ing ropes, 'sit well over the gunwale, will you? Hang on, though.' The sun suddenly disappeared and there was a noticeable drop in the temperature. Paula heard Angus swear beneath his breath. 'This is a bind,' he called out to her. 'Most unexpected. The wind was a steady force three when we started out, but never mind, we'll make it. We'll run before the wind. Sit well forward, there's a good girl, and get a good grip with your knees. Be ready to move over to the weather side if necessary.'

The wind was still rising and suddenly a gust caught them broadside on. Angus hauled on the ropes. The sails swung over and filled, and Paula felt herself rising dizzily into the air till it seemed as if she were perched on top of a high wall. She gripped hard with her knees and watched with fascinated eyes as the opposite side of the boat leaned further and further to the water. The mast tipped drunkenly over, and the straining sails swooped down and down—but just as Paula thought the boat must surely capsize, the bows made a smooth half-circle, the wall on which she crouched subsided beneath her, and they were back on an even keel. Paula saw Angus's face slide into view. He looked grim, she thought.

'Sorry about this, Paula,' he shouted above the noise of the wind and the sails. 'Are you all right?'

'Aye, aye, skipper,' she called, and cautiously relaxed her knee grip. The clouds were now spreading across the sky, and the sea was grey instead of blue. Paula gave a

little shiver. 'This damned bay,' she heard Angus muttering, and lost the rest of his remarks as another and
much stronger gust of wind caught them. It seemed to
blow from all sides at once, Paula thought, as again she
rose crazily into the air. With arms and legs tense she
watched the small craft heel over, lower and lower, till
suddenly the opposite side was actually under water.
Breathlessly she watched the swirling flood gush over,
and slap muddily about in the bottom of the boat. The
sails above her head made a terrifying arc towards the
sea. Paula waited, but just before they touched, the boat
seemed to hesitate, the sails flapped sluggishly once or
twice; then slowly, almost as it seemed, unwillingly, they
climbed again. With a slight sucking sound the boat edge
broke the water—and Paula felt herself sinking again to
her original position. But not for long. She had hardly
time to relax before the wind came at them again like a
wild creature. Up she went, clinging, clinging so fiercely
that every muscle ached.

'Paula,' she could just hear his voice above the shriek-
ing of the wind, 'I'm going to gybe. The wind's behind
us, I think, and it's our only chance. Watch the boom—
and be ready to jump if we capsize!'

'O.K.,' she yelled in reply, her staring eyes on the
helm. What happened next was so sudden that she had
no time to do anything but fling herself round, kick hard
with both feet—and take a header into the waves as far
from the toppling boat as she could get.

CHAPTER TEN

PAULA struggled to the surface and dashed the water from her eyes. She looked quickly round and saw the upturned boat with Angus's head a few yards from it. He saw her and shouted, and Paula laughed and waved an arm. Excitement took possession of her; she wanted to shout and sing.

'Paula, come and hang on,' Angus called. 'We'll soon be spotted.' He turned when he saw that she had seen him and began to swim towards the boat. Paula followed, swimming with long, leisurely strokes. What a pity we weren't both in swim-suits, she thought, heading into a white-crested wave. This is great fun. She was just a couple of yards from the boat and Angus almost there, when suddenly he seemed to falter. Paula looked at him, puzzled for a moment, then, as his head sagged sideways, she shot forward with all her strength.

'Paula!' He gave a faint despairing shout and half disappeared from view. Oh God! she thought, his heart. I must get to him. Within seconds she had reached Angus's side. She saw that his eyes were half-closed, and there was the familiar tell-tale blue ring round his lips. She grabbed him by the upper arm just in time and, turning on her back, struck out strongly with her legs, dragging the now unconscious man with her. It was only a matter of a yard or two, but Angus was a dead weight, and by the time she had reached the boat, fighting her way through the choppy seas, Paula's lungs felt like bursting. She grabbed the keel of the boat with one hand, and was just able to support Angus with the other.

Desperately she tried to shake him back into consciousness. Oh, God, help me, she prayed. If I don't get him out soon he might die.

'Help! Help!' she shrieked. The choppy waves made it difficult to see far, but Paula noticed with thankfulness that the sudden storm was already dying down. 'Help!' she shouted again. Almost at once, and to her almost hysterical relief, she heard an answering shout, and the faint beat of a motor.

Quite soon Paula saw it approaching, a large yacht with an auxiliary motor. A man and a woman were on board. 'Hold on,' the man shouted. 'We'll get you out in no time.' The motor stopped, and then Paula saw him step into the dinghy at the back of the yacht.

'Take him,' Paula gasped as he reached her side. She looked down into the pinched face lolling on her shoulder. 'He's fainted, and he has a bad heart.' Three minutes later, both she and Angus had been hauled aboard, where hot water and blankets were awaiting them. Angus soon regained consciousness, but lay on a bunk, white and shaken, and breathing with difficulty.

'Please get us to the hospital as soon as possible,' Paula begged their rescuers, trying to force some drops of hot tea between Angus's clenched teeth. 'He must have treatment.' Then she turned, the cup fell from her hand, and Paula did something she had never done before in all her healthy young life. She fainted.

After what seemed like an eternity, Paula opened her eyes and looked about her. She saw with surprise that she was in her own bed in the hospital. Frowning, she was about to sit up when Sister Leslie, in spotless white overall and head square, came softly in carrying a tray. 'Oh, hello. Awake at last?' she said, smiling.

'How long have I been asleep?' Paula asked in wonderment, then, as recollection swept over her, 'Oh—how is Angus? Is he—'

'Mr Lowther's quite all right.' Sister Leslie set down the tray and started to pour the tea. 'No need to worry at all. You fainted, you know, and I don't wonder. You still looked pretty muzzy when your rescuers brought you along in their car. D'you remember?'

Paula nodded her head. 'Yes, I do now,' she said,

raising herself on an elbow. 'Sister Leslie, is Angus—really all right? He has a strained heart, you know.'

'Yes, he told me. But it was quite a mild attack, and by last night he was almost recovered. However, I gave him a sleeping pill and kept him in bed. He seemed all right this morning.'

Paula gave a great sigh of relief, and passed a hand across her forehead. 'Oh, how glad I am to hear that,' she said. 'Now I can really enjoy this cup of tea,' and she lifted it and drank thirstily.

Mrs Leslie sat down and poured herself a cup. 'Well now, how do you feel?' she asked. 'And what happened? Oh, by the way, Mr Lowther's boat has been brought in, and no damage done, I believe.'

Paula took another long drink. 'I can still taste the sea-water,' she said with a grimace, then proceeded to give her companion a lively account of the previous day's adventure. 'I was enjoying it so much,' she said, 'and then that awful wind started. It seemed to blow all ways at once. Angus tried to gybe, but the wind veered suddenly, and over we went. I wasn't really scared, in fact I was enjoying it—till I saw what was happening to Angus, and then—well, I was, knowing what could happen. Thank God that other boat saw us when it did. I must thank them.'

'The couple came along this morning to see how you both were,' Sister Leslie said. 'They were on their way back to Hobart, but they had a chat with Mr Lowther.'

'I'm getting up,' Paula said, throwing back the bed-clothes. 'Oh, yes, I am,' as the other started to protest. 'I must have slept for hours and hours. What's the time now? Nine? Good heavens!'

'You also had a sedative,' Mrs Leslie said, smiling. 'Well, all right, if you're sure you feel well enough.'

When Paula went in to see Angus, he was up and sitting by the window. His face lit up when he saw her. 'Paula, my dear,' he said, rising and coming forward to meet her. He put both hands on her shoulders, then bent forward and kissed her cheek. 'I owe my life to you,' he said in a low voice. 'It's a debt I shall never forget. Thank you, my dear, thank you.'

Paula flushed with embarrassment and moved a pace away. 'It was nothing,' she muttered. 'I'm a pretty strong swimmer, and I learnt at school how to life-save. Anyone would have done the same. All I did was to hold you up till the other boat came.'

'And if you hadn't—' He paused, then added in a low voice, 'Come and sit down and talk to me. Are you quite all right now, Paula?'

'Yes, of course.' Her tone was a trifle impatient. All this fuss, she was thinking. I hope he's not going to start all over again. Another thought struck her. Tomorrow was her last day at Triabunna. Thoughtfully she drew up a chair and sat down beside Angus. She turned and looked at him. He was a trifle pale, but that was all.

'Angus, when are you returning to Dover?' she asked. 'You're not thinking of sailing again just yet, I hope.'

'No, I'm not,' was the sober reply. He looked tired and rather depressed, Paula thought. 'I'm going home, and I'm going to take things quietly for a bit. I hope to go tomorrow—that is, if Sister Leslie will allow me.' He grinned ruefully.

'Angus,' Paula said again, 'I don't think you should go alone—in the car, I mean. Someone who could help with the driving should be with you.'

'Oh.' He looked thoughtful. 'I suppose you're right, Paula, but—'

'I go back tomorrow too,' she remarked. 'And I can drive.'

His face cleared at once. 'Well, that's settled, then, isn't it?'

'Settled very nicely, thank you, Angus,' Paula said, smiling. 'I was getting rather tired of the coach.'

Sister Leslie passed her patient as fit to travel, and the next morning he and Paula set off. Angus was in a very quiet mood, but was obviously pleased to have her company. When they reached Hobart it was almost midday, so they drove to the hotel at Wrest Point for lunch. The waiter led them to the self-same table at which Paula and Rosalind, with Jack Sinclair and Christopher, had had dinner on their first evening in Tasmania. Paula wondered for a moment what Christopher was doing today, then quickly turned her thoughts away from him to her companion.

Angus smiled as he met her eyes. 'Paula,' he said, leaning across the table towards her, 'you asked me once why I had never married. Well, there was someone once—a long time ago.' He stopped and turned to gaze dreamily out of the window at the wide blue expanse of Sandy Bay. There was a silence, then Paula spoke.

'And what happened, Angus?' she said very softly.

He gave a short laugh. 'I was away on military service,' he said. 'When I came back she'd married some other chap.' His eyes still stared out of the wide window. 'Tame ending, isn't it?'

Paula shook her head. 'And you've never met anyone else?' she asked. He turned and looked straight into her wide hazel eyes.

'Yes, I have,' he said slowly. 'Quite recently, as a matter of fact. But—' Paula had turned her head and was now staring out at the glittering bay in her turn. Her heart was beating in a panic-stricken fashion. Angus. This was Angus speaking. Did he mean—could he mean—? But she had never thought of him in such a way. Paula had known that he was fond of her, but—well, he was—almost old. Or was he? Her eyes slid back to his face, but she saw that he was now studying the menu. No, he's not old, Paula thought with sudden surprise. In fact, Angus is a very handsome, attractive man. Suppose he asked me to—but she shied away from the question, unwilling to face it.

'Will you have a liqueur, Paula?' he asked in his normal tone, 'or just coffee?'

'Coffee, please—for both of us. Don't forget we're driving.' She smiled at him as she spoke, but found it difficult to meet his eyes.

'Then there's my heart,' he went on in a most casual

tone. 'It doesn't seem fair to—especially as she's very young.' He stopped, and Paula stared down at the table-cloth. She could feel waves of colour spreading up from her neck. Fortunately the waiter arrived at that moment with the coffee and the awkward moment passed.

'Cigarette, Paula?' Angus asked, then looked at his watch. 'We shall be at Dover in time for tea.' He paused, 'No, I don't think it would be fair on a girl—do you?'

Paula looked away from him—anywhere. What could she say in reply to his question? Nothing really; for quite suddenly and definitely Paula knew that Christopher Deane held her heart in his keeping, and that no other man would do. She might be angry, furiously angry with him on occasions, but it did not alter the fact that she loved him, completely and irrevocably. The memory of his kiss in the garden the night of the party still had power to make her shiver with ecstasy.

'I—' Paula began uneasily as the silence continued, then looked up to see that Angus was nodding and smiling in response to a boisterous greeting from a party of men at a table a few yards away.

'Are you ready, Paula?' he asked abruptly, and put out his cigarette. It was obvious to her that he did not want to get mixed up in a party, and with a sigh of relief Paula picked up her handbag.

'Quite ready, Angus,' she said, and stood up to go.

'Well, I guess Rosalind will be pleased to see you back,' he observed a little later as the car threaded its way through the busy traffic of Elizabeth Street. 'How is she getting on with her boy-friend, young Freeman?'

'I don't really know,' Paula replied, looking about her with interest; then a thought struck her. 'Angus, when we've left the traffic behind, would you like me to drive? You look tired. I should have offered before.'

'That's all right, my dear,' he said, turning to smile at her. 'I'm feeling fine, really I am. You just relax and enjoy yourself. Tell me something about your life in England.'

Paula was only too glad to comply with a request that would keep him off other subjects, so she told him all about the farmhouse in Somerset and how good Rosalind's parents had been to her. She spoke of the years of training which she and Rosalind had undergone at the big training hospital in London. Angus listened to it all with the greatest of interest. Time sped by, and then Paula saw, with pleased surprise, that they were already at Dover and the journey was over.

'Thank you for a lovely day, Angus,' she said, as he set her down at the door of the hospital. 'Sure you're all right?'

He smiled as the car moved slowly off again. 'Of course,' he said, and waved. 'I'll be seeing you again soon, I hope. Goodbye, Paula.'

She almost ran up the steps and into the hall. Everything was very quiet, but as she turned towards the door, Sister Anderson came from the direction of the dining room. She stared in surprise at Paula.

'Oh, hello, Bruce,' she said. 'We didn't expect you till tomorrow. How did you get here?'

'Mr Lowther gave me a lift. He was there for the fishing,' Paula told her. 'Where's Rosalind?'

'She's out having dinner at the local with a boy-friend. We've had only two patients in this week, and the second went out this morning, so I suggested she should go out for the evening. Did you have a good week?'

Paula picked up her suitcase. 'It had its moments,' she said, grinning and thinking of the sailing adventure, 'but there was absolutely nothing to do. Same here, apparently.'

'Till this evening,' was the reply. 'Rosalind hadn't been gone more than an hour before a baby case arrived—a Mrs Griffiths, a first. She's getting on, but very slowly. Put your case in your room, then come and have coffee in the dining room.'

'Right,' Paula said, 'and I'll get into my overall in case you need me.' She went to her room, changed, and was back within ten minutes. Betty Anderson was pouring the coffee when Rosalind came strolling in. She stopped and stared as her eyes fell upon Paula.

'Well,' she said, 'this *is* a surprise! When did you get back?' and she crossed the room and kissed Paula on the cheek.

'Hello, Ross,' Paula said giving her an affectionate squeeze. 'Half an hour ago. Angus gave me a lift back. He was in Triabunna for a few days.'

Rosalind poured herself a cup of coffee. 'What was *he* doing there?' she asked.

'He was there for the sailing and fishing.' Paula looked at Rosalind, puzzled at the withdrawn look on her face. She had been about to tell her of the sailing incident, but now she changed her mind. I'll tell her later, Paula thought. There's something wrong with Rosalind, and I must find out what it is. I do hope Philip Freeman isn't playing her up. I wonder why she's back so early. Yet she sounded perfectly all right when I rang her up at the beginning of the week.

'Why the overall?' Rosalind asked, not looking at Paula. 'I'm on tonight, you know.'

'No need for anyone to be on, as you put it,' Betty said, replacing her cup on the tray. 'Mrs Griffiths will be some time yet. I'm just going to have another look at her. Settle it between yourselves,' and she walked out of the room. There was an uncomfortable silence and Paula wondered if these two had been getting on each other's nerves, and why. She moved to Rosalind's side.

'Anything gone wrong, Ross?' she asked hesitantly. 'You—you seem—'

'Wrong?' Rosalind interrupted impatiently. 'Of course not. What makes you think—' then she suddenly stopped and put an impulsive arm round Paula's shoulders. 'I'm sorry, Paula,' she murmured. 'I'm all right, really. Don't worry. Let's both be on call, shall we? Tell me about Triabunna. Have some more coffee.'

Paula gave her a quick kiss on the cheek. She knew that it was no use pressing Rosalind, but was more than ever convinced that all was not well with her.

'How is Philip?' she asked, sitting down again at the table.

'Just as usual. He's good company.' Rosalind's tone was noncommittal as she poured the coffee. She drank it quickly, then added, 'I'll go and get into my overall just in case.'

Paula followed her in a few moments and went in search of Betty Anderson, whom she found in the patient's room. Mrs Griffiths was a thin, frightened-looking woman of about forty.

'This is Sister Bruce,' Betty Anderson said to her in a bright, conversational tone of voice, then, in a low aside to Paula, 'See if you can get her to talk. She's scared to death really, and I can't make out why. She's not young, of course, and this is her first, but everything seems to be going on O.K. Look, I'll leave you with her while I prepare the trolley.' She turned with the last words and left the room.

Paula turned and walked back to the patient. 'Are you quite comfortable, Mrs Griffiths?' she asked. 'Any pains?'

The woman on the bed stared at her with wide apprehensive eyes. 'I—I don't really know, Sister,' she whispered. 'You see, it comes and goes.'

'Well, that's all right, Mrs Griffiths,' Paula said, smiling at her. 'Are you worried about anything?'

The patient moved restlessly, avoiding Paula's eyes. 'It's not the pain,' she whispered. 'That's not much. It's—it's the worry.'

Paula sat down beside her on the bed. 'What worry?' she asked gently. 'Tell me, and perhaps I can help. Don't you—want this baby?'

The patient looked at her with large startled eyes. 'Want it!' she said. 'Why, I've wanted it for thirteen years, Sister. I couldn't believe it when it really happened. It seemed just too—wonderful to be really true.'

'Well, then?' Paula prompted, though she guessed what the trouble was.

'Sister,' Mrs Griffiths said urgently, 'I'm—I'm not

young. That's what's worrying me, and I know Jim's worried too. I'm—forty, and Jim's forty-five, Sister, I've heard that elderly parents sometimes have—' She stopped and looked at Paula.

'But you're not elderly. Forty's nothing these days. You've got to stop thinking such things. Think like this.' Paula leaned forward and smiled into the patient's face. 'I'm going to have a baby after all this time. It's happened at last. We're going to have our own child. Promise me you'll think happy thoughts. It will help you—and your baby, so much.'

Mrs Griffiths returned her smile. 'You're a pretty thing,' she said. 'I'll try, Sister, I will really.'

'That's right,' Paula said, rising and going towards the door. 'I'll be in again soon.'

At the door she met Betty Anderson. She looked heated. 'Another two cases just came in,' she whispered. 'One on top of the other. A maternity case, two weeks early, and the other's a man with what I think is an appendix. I've examined him and he seems to be in considerable pain. Will you phone Dr Renwick while I'm in with the new maternity case? How is Mrs Griffiths doing?'

'She's all right, I think,' Paula replied as she hurried off to the telephone. Rosalind came from her room as she put the receiver down.

'Anderson wants me to stay with the suspected appendix case,' she said. She grinned in her old cheery fashion, and Paula's ready smile flashed back.

'It's good to be back with you,' she said.

When Paula got back to Mrs Griffiths, she found her quiet but much more composed. Betty Anderson was sitting with her, but rose when Paula came in.

'She's being lazy,' she told Paula. 'Not getting on at all.' Rosalind appeared at the door at that moment and beckoned to her, and Betty hurried out.

Paula sat down by the bed. 'How are the pains now?' she asked.

The patient looked suddenly at her with frightened

eyes. 'They've stopped, Sister,' she said.

'D'you mean stopped completely?'

'Yes. I don't feel that I'm going to have a baby at all. Oh, Sister, do you think—' She stopped speaking and stared in a frightened silence at Paula. The latter rose and went to a cupboard.

'There's nothing to worry about,' she said reassuringly over her shoulder. 'I'll just take a reading while I'm here. Lie flat and relax, please. That's right.' There was silence as Paula placed the foetal stethoscope against the patient's abdomen. She listened carefully, moved it once or twice, then straightened up. 'There's no need to get worried, Mrs Griffiths,' she said, replacing the bed-clothes, 'but I want you to get up, put on a dressing gown and slippers and walk about the room. That will start the pains again, you'll see. Come on now, up you get.'

She waited to see the patient on her feet, then went in search of Betty Anderson. She found her in the bath-room, scrubbing up.

'How's Mrs Griffiths?' Betty asked, scrubbing away at her nails. 'Her husband's just rung up.'

Paula leaned against the doorway. 'I don't know,' she said slowly. 'I've just taken a reading. Pulse and temp are normal, but the pains have stopped completely. I don't like it, Betty.'

'Did you use the stethoscope?'

'Yes. The foetal heart is—rather faint, but the position is normal at this stage—fairly low, with the head just right, but there's hardly any dilatation. She should be having strong pains now, and she's having nothing. I've got her up, and she's walking about the room.'

There was silence for a minute or two, then Betty Anderson said, 'Dr Renwick will be here in half an hour. We'll see what he thinks. The new case has started, and Rosalind is with the appendix. You go and get something to eat and drink. We may be in for a busy night.'

Paula went off to the dining room, ate a couple of sandwiches and drank a cup of coffee before returning to

Mrs Griffiths, whom she found marching determinedly up and down the room.

'You can sit down for a while,' Paula said, smiling. 'Any signs yet?'

The patient sighed heavily and flopped on to the bed. She was about to reply when the door opened and Dr Renwick came in.

'What's all this I hear?' he said genially. 'Not getting on at all, eh? Stethoscope, please, Sister.' Paula handed it to him, and prepared the patient for his inspection.

'Hmm,' he said presently. 'No contractions at all, eh? May I see the last reading, Sister?' Paula gave it to him and he studied it for a moment in silence. 'Well now, Mrs Griffiths,' he said at last, 'Sister's going to give you something which we think will start you off again, and—' he smiled down into the pale face, 'don't worry.'

'I'll try not to.' She hesitated, then added with a rush of tears to her eyes, 'Oh, Doctor, it's not—dead, is it?'

He laid a hand on her shoulder, then said very quietly, 'Put that right out of your mind. Your baby is very much alive, Mrs Griffiths. Now get up, like a good girl, and keep on the move.'

Outside the door he said to Paula, 'Keep an eye on her, Paula, and give her a sedative.'

Paula returned to her patient and found her trailing wearily about the room. She stayed with her, chatting, for half an hour, then went to get her some tea and biscuits. 'Sit down and have this,' she said on her return. 'Any results?'

Mrs Griffiths shook her head. Poor thing, she looks exhausted, Paula thought with compassion, and went to consult Sister Anderson.

'Give Doc a ring,' said the latter, 'and tell him there's nothing doing.' Paula did so and then hurried back to Mrs Griffiths. She glanced enquiringly at her, but got a mournful shake of the head in reply.

'Can't I go to bed, Sister?' she implored. 'I feel worn out.'

'Yes, of course,' Paula replied gently. 'And I'm going

to give you something to make sure you sleep. Every-thing will be all right in the morning.' She smiled brightly at the exhausted woman, inwardly praying that her words would come true. Paula waited till she saw that the patient was well and truly asleep, then went out to see if she could help with either of the other patients. She met Betty just coming out of the sterilising room.

'My patient's doing very nicely,' the latter said in reply to Paula's question. 'No, thanks, there's nothing you can do.'

'How's the appendix case?' Paula asked. 'Can I do anything there?'

Betty Anderson looked at her in surprise. 'He's gone to Hobart,' she said. 'I thought you'd have heard the transport. Rosalind's gone with him.'

Paula stared at her. 'No, I heard nothing,' she said. 'Well—' she turned towards the dining room, 'give me a ring if you want any help, won't you?'

Dr Renwick arrived at nine the next morning and went straight to Mrs Griffiths' room. The patient was still asleep and he stood for a while studying the case sheet. 'No change at all,' he observed to Paula, who was standing at his elbow. 'Well, we'll wait till midday, and then if her condition is unchanged, we'll send her to Hobart. Might mean a Caesar. But as soon as she wakes, take another reading, and let me know at once. You'll have to take her, of course.'

CHAPTER ELEVEN

ALMOST as soon as Dr Renwick had left the patient's room she awoke, then stared, heavy-eyed, at Paula.

'How do you feel?' the latter asked, then as she did not reply, 'I've brought your tray, Mrs Griffiths. Would you like a cup of tea? Then I'm going to take another reading to see how you're getting on.'

'I'm not getting on at all,' was the dull reply. Mrs Griffiths looked at Paula, sudden panic showing in her large eyes. 'Where's Jim? Does he know about—me?'

Paula poured out a cup of tea. 'Yes,' she said. 'He telephoned last night and sent his love. He'll be ringing again this morning, I expect.' She handed the cup to the patient.

'I want to see him,' Mrs Griffiths said, taking the cup and putting it down again. 'Please, Sister, I must see him!'

'Of course you do,' Paula said soothingly. 'I'll tell him to come along. Now drink your tea while I get the things.' She went to the cupboard and took out the stethoscope and the thermometer in its glass of Dettol water. 'Ready?' she asked, rinsing the thermometer in sterile water and returning to the bedside.

The patient watched Paula's face as she bent over her. 'Is it—all right, Sister?' In her eyes was a desperate entreaty. Paula's heart almost missed a beat as she listened—and listened again. Then she raised her head and nodded.

'It's all right,' she said. 'Now drink your tea while I go to see if there's been a telephone message.'

The rest of the morning passed quietly—far too quietly, Paula thought, as she sat having an early lunch with Betty Anderson. Mrs Griffiths' condition remained unchanged, and her husband was now with her. The curtain was pushed aside and Dr Renwick came in. He looked worried.

'We won't wait any longer,' he said to Paula. 'I've told the husband, and he's going to take you both along in his car. Hobart are expecting her. I got on to them this morning. Finish your lunch, Paula, and then get the patient ready.'

It was a depressing journey that Paula, the patient and her husband took that afternoon. Try as she would Paula was unable to cheer the other two up. Mr Griffiths made one or two efforts, but it was clear that he was worried to death about his wife. Dr Renwick had had a frank talk with him, and assured him that there was nothing to fear, but Paula was moved almost to tears at the look of withdrawn misery on his face.

Mrs Griffiths held Paula's hand tightly for the whole of the journey to Hobart, and as she was carried into the hospital, she whispered to her, 'You'll come and see me, won't you?'

Paula nodded, unable to trust herself to speak. It was not that this was a new experience for her—far from it. It was the patient herself, this woman of forty who had waited and longed for a child for thirteen years. Paula had seen the incredulous joy in her eyes, and later the desperate anxiety and entreaty. It had smote upon her heart almost unbearably. 'Oh, God, let it be all right for her,' she prayed, as she walked slowly along to the Nurses' Club where she would spend the night.

Paula woke the next morning with a feeling of painful expectancy. Then she remembered. Mrs Griffiths. She must find out what had happened to her. Had she had the operation, or were they still waiting? It wouldn't be a surgical induction, she felt sure. Dr Renwick would have done that if he'd thought—Paula almost ran down the stairs to the dining room. She rapidly ate some breakfast, and then set off for the hospital. She looked at her watch as she hurried along. Yes, there was just time before she had to catch the return coach to Dover.

Paula arrived there breathless. She knew where to go

to make her enquiries, and then found herself waiting with intense anxiety for the answer to her question. The Sister in charge of the maternity wing looked at Paula in surprise, then said, 'Oh yes, of course. You're the Sister from Dover who brought the patient in, aren't you? Sister Bruce, isn't it? Well, you'll be pleased to hear that the Caesar was quite successful. The baby's a girl, and they're both doing well.'

'Oh!' Paula said faintly. She felt quite limp with relief. 'I'm *so* glad. Could I see her—just for a second?'

The other woman looked doubtful for a moment, then nodded and smiled. 'It's really only husbands,' she said, 'but I'm sure we could make an exception for you.'

When Paula came from seeing her late patient, there were tears of thankfulness in her eyes. Never had she seen such a joyous change in any woman's face, she thought, as she hurried along the corridor and made for the main entrance.

Both Mrs Griffiths and her husband had thanked her as though Paula herself had been responsible for the safe delivery of their longed-for child. 'You were so sweet and sympathetic, dear,' the mother had whispered in her ear. 'I'm glad you were with me. You'll come and see us in Dover, won't you?' and Paula had promised that she would.

She looked again at her watch. Only ten minutes before the coach left. Paula hurried her steps, and just as she was passing out of the main door, someone coming in almost collided with her. She looked up, beginning to murmur an apology, then half stopped—and looked at him.

'Good morning,' Christopher Deane said, stopping in front of her. 'How are you?'

'Very well,' Paula replied mechanically; she was breathing rather quickly. 'How are you?' She looked up at him and smiled. The joyful atmosphere of the scene she had just left still clung to her. It had brought a warm flush to her cheeks, and the light of a shared happiness shone in her clear eyes. Nothing, she felt all at once, not even a snub from Christopher, could spoil this day for her; and she smiled at him again.

'You're looking very—happy,' he said in a flat sort of voice.

'Oh, I am—I am,' Paula exclaimed impulsively, and felt all at once that she wanted to tell him—about Mrs Griffiths and her baby. 'I—' then she stopped. Something in his expression puzzled her, and before she could go on, he said,

'Yes, I can see that. You must be feeling—very relieved. Well, goodbye,' and the next moment he had disappeared into the hospital.

Paula stood still for a moment. She glanced over her shoulder in the direction of the door, then, remembering the coach she had to catch, continued on her way. What a queer, unpredictable person he is, she thought, and mentally shrugged her shoulders. He must have known about Mrs Griffiths before she spoke; and yet how gloomy he had sounded when he remarked that Paula must be very relieved. She was still puzzling over the incident as she turned into Davey Street and saw that the coach was waiting for her. Shall I ever understand him? Paula wondered. We seem now to be miles and miles apart.

Back in Dover a surprise awaited her. She found on enquiry that Rosalind had left on the morning coach for a week's holiday relief in Franklin, a small inland place about twenty miles north of Hobart.

'That was sudden, wasn't it?' Paula asked. 'Did she—like the idea?'

'I really don't know,' Betty Anderson replied. 'I didn't ask her,' and again Paula wondered what had gone wrong between these two. 'Did you see Mrs Griffiths before you left?'

Paula smiled. 'Yes, I did,' she replied. 'And oh, what a change! I've never seen anyone look so blissfully happy.'

'Yes, I can imagine. Hobart telephoned us about six this morning. Well, thank goodness that ended happily.

Doc was really worried about her. There's always the risk of waiting too long.'

'Yes, that's what I was afraid of,' Paula replied. 'Did Hobart give any particulars?'

'Oh, they said she was having quite strong contractions, but hardly any dilatation, in fact no advance on our findings. Her muscles were pretty rigid, due to her age of course, and she had a Bandl's ring. So a Caesar was the only thing, you see.'

Paula gave a sigh of content. 'Thank heaven it's all over,' she said, 'and she's got her heart's desire.'

'Come and have some lunch,' Betty Anderson said. 'You must be hungry.'

'What's doing here?' Paula asked as she sat down at the table. 'How's the other baby case?'

'Oh, everything here's just bonzer. The appendix case that Rosalind took in was operated on successfully, and Mrs West had her baby early this morning.' She yawned widely.

'Good. You must be ready for some kip,' Paula remarked, and the other girl burst out laughing.

'You're getting to be a real little Aussie,' she said. 'Yes, I'm quite ready to hand over to you. As soon as we've had lunch, I'll take you to meet Mrs West. She's a nice little person. It was her second, and the first is only just over a year old, so it was quite an easy case.'

The rest of the day and night passed quietly in the usual routine tasks, and on the following evening Rosalind telephoned from Franklin.

'Oh yes,' she replied to Paula's eager questions, 'I'm quite liking it here, though I miss the sea. How are things at Dover? Have you been out at all?'

'No,' Paula said. 'We're fairly quiet, so Betty's having a spot of leisure. She's out now.'

'Oh.' There was a pause. Paula waited, then asked, 'When will you be back, Ross?'

'End of the week, I guess. Well, 'bye, Paula, see you then.'

The next morning when Dr Renwick came in to see

Mrs West, he said to Paula, 'Like to come with me on my rounds? I think you'd find it interesting—and amusing.'

'Why, I'd love to,' Paula responded eagerly. 'I'll just go and mention it to Betty.' She hurried off, and within ten minutes she was seated beside the doctor in his shabby, well-used old car.

'Post office first,' he remarked, 'in case there's anything I can take out to my patients. Come and have lunch with Agnes and me afterwards,' he suggested. 'Lowther's coming too.'

'Thanks very much,' Paula said after a second's hesitation. 'How is Susan, by the way?'

'Very well,' Dr Renwick replied. 'Oh, she told me to tell you that if you want a sitter-in during Apple Festival, she'll be willing to oblige.'

Paula laughed. 'It's awfully good of her,' she said. 'But that isn't for some time, is it?'

'Two or three weeks; not so long.' The car began to slow down. 'Won't be a minute, Paula.' He got out and went into the post office, but reappeared almost immediately. 'Nothing,' he remarked, getting in again beside her.

'Where are we going?' Paula enquired after a few minutes. 'I'm really enjoying this.'

'I'm making for Southport. It's the other side of the bay. The road follows a sort of broad peninsula, and in places you can get a view of the sea from each side of the road. There!' He waved an arm.

'Oh, lovely!' Paula said, looking from one side to the other. 'Is there a hospital at Southport?'

'No. I have my surgery for the district there in what used to be a small hospital. Now it's used for just casualties and emergencies. There's a Sister in charge, but no beds. I suppose you'd call her a district nurse back home.' He began to slow down. 'Hello,' he called out to a couple of small boys who were capering about at the side of the road. 'Want a lift?'

'Hello, Doc,' they yelled in reply. 'Sure do.'

'And what have you two rascals been up to?' the

doctor asked as he stopped and opened the car door. The two lads, obviously brothers and aged about nine and eleven, climbed briskly in.

'Fishing,' one of them said tersely, and the other added gloomily, 'Fair cow today. You going to surgery, Doc?'

'I am,' he replied. 'But why aren't you two at school?'

'You oughter know,' the elder boy observed reproachfully. 'Our baby's got the measles.' He looked out of the window as the car began to slow down again outside a shabby little weatherboard shanty with a strip of dried-up garden in front. 'You goin' to old Pringle's?' he added, beginning to jig up and down with glee. 'You'd better watch out, Doc, 'e's got a gun.'

Dr Renwick laughed as he got out and opened the sagging gate, but as he started up the path the gangling figure of a middle-aged man appeared from round the side of the house. He carried a gun at the ready. When he saw the doctor he stopped and roared with laughter.

'O.K., Doc,' he cackled, lowering the gun and pushing a limp old felt hat to the back of his head, 'I ain't after you. It's those b——crows. Won't let my peas alone. Come on in, Doc, she's a bit better today.' He turned and led Dr Renwick into the house.

The two small boys now turned their attention to Paula. 'Someone goin' to have a baby?' one of them asked.

Paula laughed and shook her head. 'What sort of fish do you catch?' she asked.

'Gropers, mostly,' said the elder boy, and then they both burst into delighted giggles at her look of enquiry. 'Well, sometimes we get an eel,' he added. 'We'll take you if you like—one day.' Paula thanked him, and at that moment the doctor reappeared, accompanied by Mr Pringle.

'Think she'll come good, Doc?' the latter enquired casually, but with an anxious look in his eyes.

'Your wife'll be all right in a day or two,' was the cheery reply. 'Just a tummy upset, that's all it was. See that she takes the medicine I gave her. I'll call in again day after tomorrow.'

The two young passengers were dropped at the next corner, and then, after about ten minutes of steady but rather dusty driving along a straight, tree-lined road, they reached Southport. After a few minutes' drive along the quiet main road the car stopped before a small cottage-type house with a wide verandah in front. The patients, a man with a bandaged leg, two women with babies, and a small girl in charge of a dejected-looking brown dog, were gathered there. Mrs O'Rourke, the resident Sister, came out and was introduced to Paula. Dr Renwick turned to the man with the bandaged leg, and at the same moment Paula heard someone calling to her. She turned and was delighted to recognise Mrs Jones and her baby, Paula's first patients at the hospital in Dover.

'How are you, Sister?' Mrs Jones asked, as Paula came near. She indicated the baby. 'How do you think he's looking? I think he's started to teethe, so I brought him for Sister O'Rourke to look at. It's much nearer than the hospital,' she added half-apologetically. 'Oh, I'm ever so pleased to see you.'

Paula glanced into the carry-cot on the bench beside the mother. 'He's looking fine,' she said, and noticed that another car had drawn up behind Dr Renwick's. 'Early for teething, isn't it?'

'Sister Bruce, Sister Bruce!' Paula turned in surprise, and saw Hazel, Christopher Deane's little daughter, climbing out of the car and waving to her. She was closely followed by another small girl, and a middle-aged woman whom Paula recognised as the wife of the friendly man in the coach which had first brought her and Rosalind to Dover. Paula waved back, and in a few seconds there were friendly handshakes all round.

Hazel hung on to Paula's arm and said excitedly, 'I'm staying here for the week-end with Mr and Mrs Tanner. I love it here,' she gave a little skip. 'They've got lots and lots of animals, and Mandy is nearly the same age as me.'

Paula smiled at the two children and said to Hazel, 'That's nice for you,' and Mrs Tanner laughed.

'Now don't wander away,' she said to the two. 'I'm just going to see Mrs O'Rourke to get a prescription.'

'Do you work here now?' Hazel asked, looking up into Paula's face, but before she could reply, the child chattered on excitedly, 'My father's going to the mainland. He's going to be a doctor there too, an' I'm going with him.'

'Oh,' Paula said weakly. 'That's—very interesting. I—hope you'll like it there, Hazel.' It was an effort to smile into the child's welcoming face and there was a heavy weight in her breast.

'Oh, I would,' Hazel said importantly, 'except that Daddy's friend will be there too.'

'You shouldn't say things like that,' the other little girl remarked reprovingly. 'You remember what Mummy told you.'

'Oh, I don't care.' Hazel replied, tossing her flaxen plaits. 'I don't like Doreen, and she doesn't like me. I know she doesn't, but do you know who she does like? Daddy!'

'Sshh,' the other child said in a shocked voice. 'Mummy said it would be a very good thing, Hazel. You shouldn't—'

'Well, well,' it was Mrs Tanner again. 'Come along, children. Daddy's in a hurry. We mustn't keep him waiting. Goodbye, Miss Bruce. Nice to have seen you again.'

'Goodbye,' Paula murmured, hardly knowing what she was saying. 'Goodbye, Hazel. Goodbye, Mandy.' She watched the two skip down the steps and race each other to the car. Though the sun was shining as brightly as ever, all at once everything seemed dull and grey.

'Ready, Paula?' It was Dr Renwick speaking, and he looked with surprise at his companion as she turned to join him. 'You all right?' he added.

Paula nodded and smiled with a great effort. 'Of course,' she said. 'It's—hot, isn't it? Where next?'

'One more house just a little way further on, and then back home to lunch. Oh, what is it, Jenny?' this to the small girl who was pulling her depressed-looking dog towards him. She looked up at him imploringly.

'Please, Doc,' she whispered, catching at his sleeve, 'Buller ain't very well. Mum said I wasn't to come, but Sister said I could wait. Will you please give him something to make him better?'

The doctor cast a reproachful glance at Sister O'Rourke, who had just appeared in the doorway, then looked down consideringly at Buller.

'I'm not a dog doctor, Jenny,' he said mildly to the child, 'but I may have something that will do him good. Let's take him inside for a minute, shall we?'

In spite of her unhappiness Paula had to smile as Jenny, the mongrel, and the doctor disappeared into the consulting room. They reappeared in a few minutes. 'Now don't forget,' Doc called to Jenny as she started up the path, 'the other half tomorrow morning.'

'I didn't know you were a vet as well as a doctor,' Paula said, laughing, and he grinned good-temperedly.

'One learns to be a bit of everything in this job,' he said. 'Anyway, the poor kid looked so woebegone, and what I prescribed and administered won't do him any harm. By the way, young Paula, you never told me about your life-saving adventure.'

'Life-saving?' she echoed vaguely. Her thoughts were far away. Then, as she realised what he meant, 'Oh, that. I do wish Angus would forget it. He's making me into some sort of heroine, and I'm nothing of the kind.'

Dr Renwick chuckled. 'He certainly thinks the world of you, my dear,' he remarked.

Paula silently groaned, and wished that she had turned down the invitation to lunch. And half an hour later, as she greeted Susan Renwick in her home, she wished it more than ever. For there was Angus Lowther, looking very well indeed and advancing towards Paula with outstretched arms.

'Here's my little heroine,' he said, kissing her on the

cheek. 'If it hadn't been for her, I wouldn't be here now.'

Paula looked at the grinning face of Frank Renwick and burst out laughing. 'Look, Angus,' she said, 'I know you're grateful and all that, but please let it rest now. Let's talk of something else.'

Dr Renwick winked at his wife. 'Let's *do* something else,' he suggested. 'Come on, folks, let's eat.' And he led the way into the dining room.

The meal passed pleasantly enough, though Paula had to make a great effort to appear as usual. She was secretly grateful when Angus suggested as soon as the meal was over that he should run her back to the hospital. He seemed to sense that she was not feeling her normal bright self, and did not worry Paula with overmuch talk.

'And how's Rosalind?' he asked just before stopping at the hospital door.

'Very well,' Paula replied. 'She comes back the day after tomorrow. Goodbye, Angus, thanks very much for the lift.'

He seemed to hesitate for a brief moment, then smiled and drove away.

As Paula walked up the steps she heard the telephone ring, and then Betty Anderson's footsteps in the hall. 'Just in time,' she said to Paula as she came in. 'It's for you. Had a good time?'

Paula smiled and nodded as she took the receiver from her hand.

'Hello, that you, Paula?' It was Rosalind's voice. Paula's spirits lifted.

'Ross!' she said eagerly. 'How nice. How are you?'

'All right.' There was a pause. 'Listen, Paula, I've something to tell you. I wondered at first if I should wait till I got back, but—'

'Ross,' Paula interrupted, 'what—what is it? What's gone wrong?' Rosalind's voice had sounded—queer, she thought. 'Are you—'

'I'm all right.' The voice was impatient. 'But listen, someone has turned up. I expect you can guess who I mean.' There was a pause, then Paula said very quietly, 'D'you mean—Bob?'

'Yes.'

Paula's heart seemed to stop beating. Bob—back in Tasmania! And suddenly she wanted to laugh. What a day it had been! Surely nothing else could happen. She cleared her throat.

'Ross,' she said rather huskily, 'when—and where did you see him?'

'I haven't seen him, Paula. But listen. The day before I arrived there was a car accident, and Bob was brought in. What? No, of course not. Listen, Paula, he was taken to the hospital in Hobart to be operated on. Now, I admitted a patient today and saw his name in the book. I made enquiries, and—it's him, Paula.' A pause. 'Paula, are you still there?'

Paula licked suddenly dry lips. 'Yes,' she said. 'Go on, Ross. Have you heard—how he is?'

'Yes. I got chatting with the other Sister here, without letting her know I knew him, of course, and she told me that he's getting on all right.'

Paula sat down suddenly on the chair nearby. A wave of relief swept over her. After all, she had loved Bob once, or had thought she did.

'Paula,' it was Rosalind's voice again, 'don't let it upset you, will you? And—you won't do anything about it?'

There was a brief pause, then Paula said slowly, 'I don't know, Ross. I think—I shall probably go to see him. I feel, somehow, that I should.'

CHAPTER TWELVE

PAULA walked slowly to her room. She felt quite numb after the events of this day which had started in so pleasant a fashion. Almost mechanically she took off her summer frock, washed her hands and face, and put on a crisp white overall. Well, she thought as she tucked a stray lock of hair under her cap, I've certainly got what Doc would described as "plenty on my plate". And Christopher, what of him? Paula wondered unhappily if she would ever see him again. Then there was Doreen. Were they really engaged? Everything seemed to point that way. And yet—she stopped pinning her cap and stared into the mirror. Christopher had liked her, she knew; and such a short time ago. It was Bob, this man she was going to visit, who had started the endless trail of misunderstandings; and it had gone on, getting worse and more complicated and hopeless.

Paula sighed and turned to the door. It was not only Bob, she knew that. Her own stupid pride was partly to blame. She had been hurt and angry at Christopher's attitude, and she had cause. But, and she sighed again, it was not the way to clear the air between them. Was it too late even now? Paula wondered. Could she sink her own pride and break through this web of misunderstanding? She shrugged her shoulders wearily. She wasn't even sure now that Christopher was interested.

And now Bob was back. To complicate matters even more? She just didn't know. He might have changed in these four months. After all, he hadn't written again, and she herself had almost forgotten that he had said that he intended seeing her again when next his ship was in Hobart. Well then, wasn't she being foolish in going to see him in hospital? Paula walked along the passage and into the small office. But I'd feel mean if I didn't, she

141

thought rather unhappily. After all, he's a fellow countryman in a strange country. I must know that he *is* all right. Ross will think I'm quite mad, I know, but— Paula's thoughts paused for a moment as she considered this point. But would she? She hadn't said much against it really. Paula went over their telephone conversation in her mind, and decided that, rather surprisingly, Rosalind had said very little to dissuade her.

There was no one in the office and Paula wandered through to the kitchen. Minnie was at the window shelling peas and throwing an occasional titbit out to Dilly the duck, who now had a husband to keep her company.

'She's getting that cheeky,' Minnie observed, aiming a pea at the waiting duck; then, looking at Paula, she added, 'Sister's upstairs with the new patient.'

'New patient?' Paula echoed. 'When—'

'Came in just before dinner,' Minnie said, tipping the pea shucks into a bucket. 'Nice young feller.'

'Well, I'd better go and see if I'm needed,' Paula murmured, and went in search of Betty Anderson. She found her in the sluice, packing one of the drums.

'Hello,' said Betty, when she saw Paula's face at the door. 'New patient in.'

'Yes, Minnie told me. What's the matter with him?'

Betty banged down the lid of the drum. 'I wouldn't know till Doc comes in,' she said, 'but I'm almost certain it's kidney trouble. He's having a lot of pain high up in the back, and the specimen seems to confirm it. I've just phoned Doc, and he's coming along. Will you look in on Mrs West and see that the baby takes its feed? She's a dinkum kid, but a nuisance over her feeds; hardly took any at the ten o'clock.'

'Yes, all right,' Paula said, and as she went towards Mrs West's room, she heard Dr Renwick's car coming up the drive.

Later on in the afternoon, as the three of them sat over cups of tea, the doctor, who was looking thoughtful, said to Sister Anderson, 'I think you're right about young Jim Foley, but of course we can't start treatment till we get the analyst's report. The specimen has gone, I suppose?' She nodded to his look of enquiry. 'Give him fifteen milligrams of pethedine tonight, but don't start a special diet till we get the positive. Should be tomorrow or the next day. A little something to help him sleep would be a good thing. Mrs West goes out tomorrow, doesn't she?'

'Yes,' Betty Anderson replied. 'The baby's difficult to feed, but I've told her she must persevere. She's got plenty, and I've shown her what to do.'

'Good.' Frank Renwick rose to his feet. 'By the way, Paula,' he turned to her with a grin on his face, 'you'll be pleased to hear that Buller has recovered. I met Jenny with him in the village. Castor oil's wonderfully effective, you know.'

The next day passed in quiet routine duties. Mrs West and the baby were called for by a proud father, and Jim Foley, now the only patient, seemed easier, and slept peacefully for most of the day. Betty Anderson went out to spend the evening with Frank and Susan Renwick.

Paula had just been in to see that the patient was quite comfortable when the telephone rang. Minnie had left for home, so Paula went to answer it. It was Rosalind.

'Hello, Paula,' she began, 'I thought you'd like to know that our friend is recovering. Yes. I heard from a girl here who is pally with the Sister in charge of his ward. She thinks he's very attractive, by the way.'

'I'm very glad, Ross,' Paula said quietly. 'Thanks for letting me know, chum.'

'Here's another bit of news that might interest you,' Ross went on.

Paula felt a sudden coldness at her heart. Was Ross going to tell her that Christopher and Doreen were to be married? She waited breathlessly.

'It's about—you know—your second string.' Paula frowned. There was a hard flippancy about Rosalind these days that she did not very much like. But she said nothing and waited. 'You still there, Paula? Oh, I just wondered. Well, apparently, *he* is going to the mainland, to join the Flying Doctor Service.'

There was a pause.

'Oh,' Paula said at last. 'That's—definite, is it?'

'Yes, quite. Paula, about Bob. Will you—still go to see him?'

'Yes.' Paula's voice was brief. 'Look, Ross, I'll have to go now. Thanks for telling me. See you tomorrow.'

Paula returned to her patient in a thoughtful mood. For the first time in her life she was seriously at odds with Rosalind, and she did not know why.

However, the next midday, when Rosalind returned from Franklin, she appeared to be in very good spirits. She greeted Paula affectionately, and the latter wondered, in a puzzled fashion, if she had been wrong about her. The evening passed pleasantly; Betty Anderson was with the one and only patient, and Paula and Rosalind lingered comfortably over their coffee in the dining room.

'Philip came over to Franklin one day,' Rosalind remarked. 'We went boating on the lake. More coffee, Paula?'

'Yes, I'll have another cup. Oh, there goes the telephone. I'll go,' and Paula hurried out into the hall.

'Hello. That you, Paula?' It was Miss Needham's voice. 'How are you? Good. Now, how many patients have you there? Only one? Well now, look here, my dear, I want you in Hobart for a week at least. This is the position. Two Sisters who are coming here from the mainland have been delayed. A Sister here, on the permanent staff, has gone down with fever, and two others are due for holidays which have already been postponed once. D'you see? Now we don't usually call upon the Tourist Nursing Service, but under the circumstances there's no alternative. I want you here tomorrow, Paula. That all right? Good. Now, I'd like to speak to Sister Anderson, please. Goodbye, my dear. Come and see me, won't you?'

Paula called to Betty Anderson whom she knew was in the office. 'Miss Needham,' she said. 'She wants to speak to you,' and handed her the receiver. Rosalind followed

Betty and looked enquiringly at Paula.

'Well, it's me this time,' Paula said to her. 'Never a dull moment, is there?'

'Where?' Rosalind asked, and raised her eyebrows significantly when Paula told her.

'Looks as if fate intends you to meet up again with a certain person,' she said in a low tone.

Paula gave her a puzzled look. 'It's only because I feel I ought to go,' she said, and they were joined that moment by Betty Anderson.

'This is most unusual,' she said to Paula. 'The Royal Hobart has its own staff, and they make their own arrangements for reliefs, and so on. They certainly *must* be in a spot to call on the Tourist people.'

'I don't see why they shouldn't,' Rosalind said.

'Except that they never do,' the other retorted.

That night Rosalind came into Paula's room as she was packing her suitcase ready for the journey to Hobart the next morning.

'Hello, Ross,' Paula said, sitting back on her heels before the open case. 'Throw over that housecoat, will you?'

'Paula.' Rosalind picked up the garment from the bed and folded it slowly. Paula looked at her in surprise and waited.

'Yes?' she prompted at last. 'What is it, Ross?'

A flush rose to Rosalind's cheeks. 'There's something more I ought to tell you.' She looked down at the folded garment in her hands, then shook it out again. 'It's—about Bob.' She paused, then went on speaking. 'He told the Sister at Franklin that at the time of the accident he was looking for—a friend.'

Paula stared at Rosalind, then slowly got to her feet. 'Why didn't you tell me that before?' she asked.

'I—forgot.' The colour deepened in her round cheeks and she looked away from Paula. 'Don't go to see him, Paula,' she said suddenly. 'It'll only—'

'But, Ross,' Paula interrupted impatiently, 'that's silly, and you know it is. If Bob is still trying to find me, and he's there in the hospital where I'm to be for a week or more—well, he's almost certain to find out. In any case, I feel it would be most unkind not to go near him. And after all, Bob can't make me do anything I don't want. Of course I shall go to see him.'

'Oh well,' Rosalind shrugged her shoulders, then, looking down at the housecoat she still held, 'on your own head be it,' and tossed it into the case. Paula smiled at her as she turned again to her packing.

'You know,' she said, wrapping paper round a pair of shoes, 'my ex-fiancé is not the sort to sigh indefinitely over one girl. He'll give up—in time.' Then, to change the subject, she added, 'Seen anything of Philip lately?'

Rosalind laughed and sat down on the bed. 'No,' she said. 'I don't think Betty approves of him—or me, either.' Paula looked at her in dismay. 'Ross, what's the matter between—' she was beginning, when she heard Betty's footsteps approaching her room.

'Are you there, Rosalind?' Betty called, and Rosalind grimaced at Paula and got to her feet.

'Don't worry,' she said to her as she went out. 'Tell you later. It's nothing really.'

But Paula's time of departure came without an opportunity arising. The latter worried a little, but as she noted what excellent spirits Rosalind appeared to be in as she waved goodbye, Paula tried to dismiss it from her mind for the time being at least.

All the way to Hobart her thoughts turned continually to Bob Shaw. In spite of her confident words to Rosalind Paula was not at all sure that she was acting wisely in going to visit him. There was the danger that he would misconstrue it. On the other hand, as she had said to Rosalind, it would be an easy matter for him to find out where she was. No, Paula decided at last; as Bob had turned up again, and would most certainly be in Hobart for some weeks, it was better to get the situation clear between them. Paula felt much happier after this decision had been made.

After settling in at the Nurses' Club, Paula started her

duties at the Royal Hospital, Hobart. For the first day she worked with the Sister she was relieving in Tasman Ward, men's surgical. Her heart had leapt uncontrollably when first she heard that it was to be a surgical ward. Would she see anything of Christopher, Paula wondered, or was he away just at present? Well, she would soon know. But when the permanent Sister had gone, and Paula was studying the case sheets and charts, she saw with bitter disappointment that none of Tasman Ward cases were his. But he can't have gone yet, she thought, and felt that she must find out somehow. However, Paula was saved the trouble of finding out by Staff Nurse Elliott of Tasman Ward, who was a born chatterbox.

Paula had not been on her own in the ward more than half a day before she knew that Mr Deane's cases were all in Allonah Ward, which was on the next floor; that they were the more serious surgical cases, and that her friend, Nurse Scott, in Allonah, said that everyone there was ever so sorry that Mr Deane was leaving.

As Paula surveyed the long ward on that first day it was like a return to St Just's. All the beds were occupied, and the double row seemed to stretch into an endless distance. It felt strange to her, but after the second day she found that she had slipped effortlessly into the familiar hospital routine. It started with the careful reading of Night Sister's report. Washings, bed-making, temperatures and breakfasts had all been completed before the day staff came on duty. And now came doctor's rounds.

Paula looked up as the door opened, then moved quickly forward. It was the visiting surgeon accompanied by the houseman. With them, somewhat to her surprise, was Matron; and then Paula saw that it was Miss Norris who had interviewed her at Tasmania House in London, nearly six months ago. Now she smiled and spoke a few friendly words as Paula took her place behind the houseman. Staff Nurse Elliott, wheeling a trolley covered with a white cloth, fell in behind Paula, and two young probationer nurses brought up the rear.

Slowly the cavalcade moved from bed to bed. The surgeon spoke a few words to each patient, then looked at the chart which Paula had placed ready for him. Once he asked for Night Sister's report, and studied it closely. At one bed he asked for the dressings to be removed from a double hernia case, and while Staff Nurse quickly wheeled the trolley into position, the two probationers put up the screens. When, eventually, the last bed had been visited, and Matron and the two doctors had gone, then it was time for Paula, the staff nurse, and the probationers to go round again with drugs and dressings trolley and attend to each patient. After that came a brief lull, then dinner, which Paula and the other three took round. The afternoon was even busier than the morning. After a short rest, the patients were washed, temperatures and pulses taken, and then beds made. Visiting time was after the patients' high tea which was served from half-past five to six. Promptly at that time relations and friends poured into the ward, and with a sigh of relief Paula retired to the small ward office, where Staff Nurse Elliott brought her a cup of tea.

Paula's last duty of the day was to accompany the staff nurse as she wheeled round the trolley containing sedatives and laxatives. At one bed, occupied by a lanky Australian with a leathery face and a merry eye, Paula, who had lingered for a few minutes at the double hernia case, heard a short interchange between him and Staff Nurse Elliott.

'Aw, come on, Nursie,' she heard the patient say. 'What about one of them blue pills tonight? Had a green one yesterday. Didn't do me no good. Blue's my colour. It suits me eyes.'

'Maybe,' was the answer, 'but you'll have a green one just the same.'

'Aw well,' in a resigned tone, then, his eyes lighting on Paula, 'Say, Nursie, who's the new Sister? She's a little beaut. Wouldn't mind taking her out—'

'Quiet!' hissed Nurse Elliott. 'She'll hear you. Anyway, she wouldn't go out with you, Bill Nolan.'

The patient shook his head sadly. 'Too true she wouldn't,' he agreed. 'Now, how about you?'

Paula, finding it difficult not to laugh, moved out of earshot, and so did not hear Nurse Elliot's response to this invitation.

On the third day of her stay in the Royal Hospital, Hobart, Paula had seen nothing of Christopher, though she knew that he visited Allonah almost every day, in the mornings. Staff Nurse Elliott had supplied this information. On the evening of the fourth day, after Paula came off duty, she decided to visit Bob. She had been putting it off till her own ward had afternoon visiting instead of evening; which was three times a week. It meant that Paula was off duty earlier than other days, and so could visit Allonah at the proper time.

Allonah Ward looked exactly like Tasman, Paula thought as she paused at the entrance. There were the same groups of friends and relatives gathered round the various beds. Her heart was beating apprehensively as she glanced down the long room. Halfway down on the right side Paula saw one bed with no one near it, and as she recognised Bob's fair head bent over a newspaper, she was suddenly glad that she had come. He looked lonely and bored, and only looked up from the paper when he heard her stop beside his bed. He stared at her for a moment unbelievingly, then, 'Paula!' he almost shouted, and held out both hands to her.

Paula felt all her doubts disappearing at the gladness which shone in his face. She felt that, come what may, she had been right in coming to see him.

'Hello, Bob,' she said, and sat down beside him. 'How are you?'

'Paula!' He grasped both her hands in his. 'This is wonderful. Did you—have you—come to see me?'

Paula laughed at his incredulous face. 'Yes, of course. I heard about your accident, so naturally I came to see how you were getting along. I brought you these,' and she laid a basket of fruit on the bedside locker.

Bob stared at her. 'Gosh, Paula,' he said. 'Here, let me have a good look at you.' He reached for her hands and pulled her towards him. Paula laughed a trifle nervously; and at the same moment a voice behind her said,

'And how is my patient this evening?'

Paula stiffened where she sat. With a horrible sense of fatefulness she knew who was there, watching her and Bob. It would be Christopher Deane, of course. He seemed to have an uncanny knack of turning up at the wrong moments, Paula thought; even at visiting time, though she supposed he knew that Bob was not likely to have friends visiting him. She stood up slowly and turned to look at him. He was wearing loose informal sports clothes and was alone, obviously on a casual visit. But why, Paula thought with exasperation, did it always have to happen like this?

'Good evening, Miss Bruce,' Christopher said, and smiled at her quite charmingly. But before Paula could reply, he turned to Bob and said, 'Well, I won't stay this evening as I see you have a visitor, and a very charming one, too. Feeling all right?'

The patient gave him a delighted smile. 'You bet,' he said fervently. Christopher smiled rather stiffly in reply, half-bowed to Paula, then turned and went back down the crowded ward. Paula resumed her seat.

'He's a good chap,' Bob remarked, jerking his head towards the receding figure. 'Been darned good to me, and you know,' he gave Paula a rather sheepish grin, 'I felt a bit ashamed. Y'see, I recognised him. He was at Wrest Point that night when I met you, wasn't he? I don't think he remembers me. Good thing, too. I wasn't at my best that night, was I? I'm sorry about that, Paula.'

She gave a slightly embarrassed laugh. 'Forget it,' she said. 'I have.' And then wondered uneasily if she had said the wrong thing. She must not give Bob false hopes, Paula thought.

'Come a bit closer,' Bob said. 'Tell me all about yourself. Aren't you going to give me a kiss, Paula?'

'Oh, Bob,' she said, suddenly wanting to laugh at him,

'you're hopeless!' From the corner of her eye Paula had seen that Christopher had slowed down and was probably watching them. He might even have heard Bob's words, for he had a very penetrating voice. 'How long are you going to be in hospital?' she asked.

'I wouldn't know,' was the cheerful reply. His eyes slid towards the door, and hers followed. Christopher had disappeared. 'Anyway, I can't leave Tassie till I'm appointed to another ship,' Bob continued. 'Perhaps not even then,' and he gave Paula a quick glance. 'D'you know,' he reached forward and took her hand, 'I was trying to find you when the accident happened. Someone said they thought you were at Franklin. They said there was an English Sister who hadn't been out from home very long.'

'They must have meant Rosalind,' Paula murmured, drawing her hand from his. She saw his eyes go again towards the door, and wondered if, after all, Bob was expecting a visitor. Something about him was puzzling her. He looked very well, she thought, and was obviously making rapid progress. But apart from all this, there was an air of expectancy about him. Paula hoped again uneasily that she had not given him the wrong idea.

'Well, anyway,' Bob said, bringing his gaze back to her, 'here you are now, and I'm very glad to see you. How are you liking Tasmania now? Not sorry you left England?'

Paula shook her head, smiling. 'No, oh, no,' she said. 'I love it.'

'I agree with you,' Bob said dreamily. 'I think it's a wonderful country—with some wonderful people in it,' and again, at a sudden movement from the door, his eyes slid quickly in that direction. This time they remained fixed. Paula stared at him for a moment, puzzled at his tone, then quickly she also glanced towards the door. A young girl, very pretty, and in probationer's uniform, had just entered. As Paula watched, the girl's eyes darted towards Bob's bed, and she smiled shyly at him.

Paula looked quickly at Bob, and was in time to note the almost fatuous expression of devotion on his face. She lowered her own eyes, her first feeling being one of relief for herself and gladness for Bob. Then her lips twitched and she wanted badly to laugh. I needn't have worried, she thought, and stood up.

'Well, I must go now, Bob,' she said. 'But I'll be in again to see you. Get well soon.'

'I will,' he replied almost absently, eyes on the slim, slowly advancing figure, then, with an effort, 'Thanks for coming, Paula. I'll see you again.'

Paula turned to go, then smiled at the young nurse who was now near Bob's bed. She's certainly very pretty, she thought, and as she passed through the door of Allonah Ward, well, thank goodness, one problem at least is solved. Paula had a strong desire to laugh at herself. You're too conceited, she thought. I wonder what Ross will say when I tell her that Bob is in love again?

CHAPTER THIRTEEN

WHEN Paula got back to the Nurses' Club that evening she kicked off her shoes, took a bath, and changed into a cool, comfortable housecoat. She had had a tiring day, and the meeting with Bob in the evening had been a strain—to begin with, but not for long. Her lips curved up again in a smile as she thought of the latest development in that quarter. Well, that business was settled, she thought; and by Bob himself, too. She sank, with a sigh of relief, into an easy chair. It was pleasant to think that she had nothing more to worry about where he was concerned, and also that Bob himself was happy. Paula's thoughts moved on to Christopher Deane and she sighed impatiently. Of course, he had seen Bob holding both her hands in his, and later had almost certainly heard his words. Fate seems determined to give Christopher a wrong impression of me, she thought, but before she could pursue this subject there was a knock at her door.

'Come in,' Paula called, wondering who it could be. Miss Needham opened the door, and came in.

'Ah, there you are!' she said as Paula rose quickly to her feet. 'No, no, my dear, I can't stay,' as the latter pulled forward a chair. 'I just dropped in to talk about tours. I wondered if you and—what's her name? Rosalind—would like a trip to the islands next month. Two of the girls over there are due for leave. I could manage to send you together, I think.' She looked across at Paula, and added quickly, 'Anyway, think it over. But there's always great competition for the Island hospitals, so if it doesn't attract, don't hesitate to say so.' She turned towards the door. 'What about having supper with me one evening before you go back?'

'I'd love to,' Paula said, accompanying her to the door.

'Tomorrow?' Miss Needham suggested, and Paula smiled and nodded.

'Thank you,' she said. 'I shall look forward to it.'

The following evening when she came off duty, Paula remembered that Mrs Griffiths, the Caesar case from Dover, would be still in the maternity wing, so, instead of going back to the Club, she went along to see her. She found Mr Griffiths with his wife, and the two gave her a great welcome. The baby, a fine little girl, was shown off by the proud parents, and duly admired by Paula. She spent a happy half hour with the little family, then walked back to the club to make ready for the visit to Miss Needham. The rest of the evening passed pleasantly looking at the photographs and postcards of the "inland" which she had in various albums and boxes. There were pictures also, of Alf Traeger, the inventor of the first pedal wireless, with the early versions of this ingenious device.

'He's improved it enormously, of course,' Miss Needham said. 'Now practically all the outback stations have their transceivers. And this,' pulling a large photograph from underneath a pile of others, 'is John Flynn, who inspired Alf Traeger. The dream of John Flynn's life was a Flying Doctor service to link up all the lonely stations of the inland. He never let up, and eventually he and Traeger between them made the dream a reality. Flynn started the service, and Traeger's transceivers made the link-up possible. This is a picture of John Flynn, taken just before he died.'

'It's a wonderful service,' Paula said softly, studying the two photographs.

'Yes, it is indeed,' Miss Needham replied, then added, 'Did you know that our Mr Deane is joining it?'

Paula's heart leapt at the sudden reference. 'Yes,' she said, trying to sound casual, 'I had heard. Why is he making this change, I wonder?'

Miss Needham began to tidy a box of postcards. 'He's wanted to for a long time,' she remarked. 'Ever since that tragedy about his wife, you know. But it's only lately that it's cropped up again. I thought he'd got over it, and was settling down.'

Paula's heart was beating faster than usual. Evidently Miss Needham thought that Paula knew about this "tragedy". She waited.

'But perhaps it's the best thing for him,' Miss Needham went on in a thoughtful tone of voice. 'It must have taken a lot of living down.'

Paula looked at her, then said rather breathlessly, 'Miss Needham, I—I hadn't heard about Mr Deane's wife. I knew he was a widower, but that's all.'

Miss Needham stopped her tidying and stared at Paula. 'Oh dear,' she said, 'I never thought that—anyway, it's pretty well known, and you'd have heard sooner or later. It all happened five years or more ago. His wife ran away with another man. She was a beautiful girl, but everyone knew that she led Mr Deane a dog's life.'

'So he—he's not really a widower, then,' Paula said quietly. Miss Needham shook her head sadly.

'It was a terrible tragedy. Oh yes, he's a widower all right. You see, the wife and the other man were killed in a plane crash only a week later. Poor Mr Deane, it must have been an awful shock, the one following so quickly on the other. I've heard that he adored her. It's made a great change in him, too. He used to be such a gay, friendly person. Now—well, I sometimes think he doesn't trust anyone.'

'Oh, how dreadful!' Paula said, her voice not quite steady. 'I can understand that. But—' she hesitated, then went on, 'I have heard that—well, there's a rumour that he's marrying again.' She waited breathlessly, hoping against hope that Miss Needham would know something definite.

'Yes, I've heard that,' was the reply, 'and I've seen him out with quite a pretty, smart-looking girl. I only hope it's true. He needs a wife, and Hazel, the child, needs a mother.'

'Yes, I suppose so,' Paula agreed after a pause. So

Miss Needham knew no more than anyone else. Soon after that she said goodnight to her hostess, and started for home. But halfway there she changed her mind and turned again into Collins Street. The conversation with Miss Needham had left Paula in a state of unrest, and she felt she needed space to think things over. What she had heard of Christopher's private life had shed a new and unexpected light upon him. Paula felt now that she could understand him better. Hadn't she herself, after the unhappy affair with Bob Shaw, felt that she could never trust another man? Then how much more a husband with an adored wife.

She walked quickly in the direction of the harbour, then turned towards Battery Point. She reached the promenade and stood leaning her elbows on the rail. It was a lovely cool evening after the hot, busy day. The sun was setting over Sandy Bay, and the sky was a glory of pinks, greens, and gold. A gentle breeze blew Paula's hair back from her brow as she stared dreamily out at the anchored ships. Her thoughts turned to Bob and she half-smiled. At least everything was turning out well for him. There had been no mistaking the look on his face, or on that of the young girl either. They were in love, with eyes for no one but each other. She wondered now if Bob was planning to stay and settle in Tasmania. The breeze was turning chilly and Paula gave a sudden shiver. And as she turned to go back, her thoughts went back to Christopher.

She was seized suddenly with bitter regret she hadn't been bold enough to shape the pattern of the last few months. She could have done it, she felt, if only she had been willing to sink her own pride. She looked up, and as if in answer to her unhappy musings, a car came along the promenade, going slowly in the direction of Collins Street. Paula looked quickly away, but not before she had recognised Christopher Deane and his companion, Doreen. The girl was sitting very close to him, and looking up into his face, and they were both laughing. They did not see Paula, for which she was glad as she lowered her head and turned away. It's a good thing for me that he's going, she thought bleakly. I suppose I ought to be glad to see him laughing, and seeming so happy, but what I really wish is that I were there in her place, sitting close beside him and watching the smile of happiness on his face.

Paula stared straight ahead, and did her best to forget those two smiling faces. Was I mistaken in thinking he liked me quite a lot? she wondered, then: Well, even if I were not, this other girl seems to have made the running while I've sat back and done nothing. And now it's too late. Perhaps I did make a mistake. After all, I was mistaken about Bob; maybe it's the same with Christopher. Maybe I'm wasting my time. But this sensible reasoning did not make her feel any happier.

The next day ran its usual course; perhaps it was even busier than usual. Paula had thought of visiting Bob again in the evening as she now had only two more days left in the hospital. But at the end of the day, as she handed her report to Night Sister, Paula felt that all she wanted was a hot bath, a meal and bed. She'd go to see Bob tomorrow, she decided. As she came out of the big main entrance, Paula glanced at the kerb, and saw Christopher sitting at the wheel of his car. She looked quickly the other way, and started off for McQuarrie Street. But she had not gone more than a few paces before she heard a car draw up beside her.

'Miss Bruce,' Christopher called, 'do let me offer you a lift.' Paula stopped and faced him as he got out and opened the near side door. She was feeling curiously numb. 'You look very tired,' he said quite gently. 'Where are you going? Can't I take you there?'

'I'm going to the Club,' Paula said stiffly, and thinking of his face as he had looked at Doreen. 'And I can quite easily walk, thank you. It's not far.'

Christopher hesitated, looking at Paula's unresponsive face, then he suddenly smiled. 'I'd *like* to take you along,' he said. 'Won't you give me that pleasure?'

Paula went towards the car without looking at him.

Her heart was beating in heavy thuds against her chest. Christopher closed the car door and went round to the other side. There was silence as the car moved smoothly off, then presently he said, 'You'll be leaving here soon, I suppose?'

'Yes,' Paula said briefly. Black depression had descended upon her and she felt she wanted to cry. She dared not look at Christopher. He was the man she loved, but they had never been farther apart than they were at this moment. Oh, I wish I'd never met him, Paula thought, and tried to still the trembling of her lips. He's just being kind, that's all, and I can't bear it. With mouth fiercely compressed she stared out of the window and saw that they were already in McQuarrie Street.

'I hear that you're leaving Tasmania,' she said, making a desperate effort at composure, and giving him a quick side-glance.

'Yes, in about two months' time,' Christopher replied in a pleasantly formal voice. 'I shall be sorry in many ways to leave Tassie, but the job I'm going to is something I've wanted to do for a long time, and now the chance has come along. I'm joining the Flying Doctor Service on the mainland.'

'Yes, I heard.' She saw that they had nearly reached the club, and the car was slowing down. 'Well, thank you for the lift,' Paula said rather breathlessly, 'and congratulations on the new job—and the best of luck for the future.'

The car stopped, and there was a short silence between the two. Then Christopher got out and opened the door for Paula. She got out, and half turned to say goodnight, but he took her by the elbow and accompanied her to the porch. Paula began to tremble as he drew her into the shadows there. He released her arm and stood facing her, then gently raised her face with one finger.

'Thank you for your good wishes,' he said. 'Goodnight, Paula, and I hope you'll be very, very happy.'

Suddenly and briefly she felt his lips on hers, and then he was gone.

Paula turned quickly. She was bewildered and dazed, but no longer as depressed as she had been. But even as she took a swift pace forward she heard the sound of the car starting up. It was too late to say or do anything, but—he had kissed her. Still feeling dazed she turned to go in. Christopher's kiss this time had been gentle, almost—yes, regretful, and he had hoped she'd be *very* happy. And suddenly Paula wondered just why he had said that. Why, just at this moment, should he hope that she would be very, very happy? It was almost as if she, and not he, were going away to start a new life. Paula puzzled over this point for a few moments, then decided that there was really no significance in it. I'm just clutching at straws, she thought miserably.

At supper that evening Paula met another girl who belonged to the Tourist Division. They got talking together and the other girl was very interested to hear that Paula was doing duty at the Royal Hobart Hospital. 'You're lucky,' she said. 'We don't often get a chance of the big hospitals.'

'I suppose I am,' Paula replied, 'but I think I prefer the small ones. It's like being in one's own home, don't you think? What are the islands like? I might do a tour on one of them fairly soon.'

'Oh, they're bonzer.' The other girl's voice was most enthusiastic. 'I was at King Island about a year ago. I loved it.'

But Paula's attention was already straying. She could think of nothing but the recent encounter with Christopher. After puzzling once more over his words, she had reluctantly come to the conclusion that what he meant was that she would be very happy during her tour of service in Tasmania—and that was all. A kind of last good wish, Paula thought, and sighed. She said goodnight to her companion, and went to bed.

'Sister, do you know Nurse Scott in Allonah?' Staff Nurse Elliott asked Paula the next morning. Doctor's rounds were over, and now the two of them were starting off with the loaded D. and D. trolley to visit each patient in the long ward. Paula gave the girl a quick glance, and saw that she was watching for her reaction to this question. So she knows about my visit to Bob, Paula thought with a half-smile.

'I don't think so,' she said, 'unless—is she a pretty blonde girl with brown eyes?'

'That's her—a real beaut she is. Well, she's fallen for that Merchant Navy chap in there.'

'Oh, really?' Paula said, and stopped at the first bed. 'Screens, please, Nurse,' she said, turning to one of the probationers. 'Well, how are you this morning, Mr Weston?'

The patient, a youth of about twenty who had had an operation for a cracked knee-cap, grinned at her anxiously.

'I'm O.K., Sister,' he assured her. 'But when'll I be able to play football again?'

'Oh, you must ask the doctor that question,' Paula replied. 'Swab, please, Nurse. Anyway, it's doing very nicely,' she added, smiling down into his flushed face. 'You'll just have to be patient.'

'Yes, Sister,' the youth murmured submissively. 'But I feel I could get up right now. Pukka dinkum, Sister.'

Paula smiled. 'I'm glad to hear it,' she said. 'But pukka dinkum or not, you're to stay right there, and do as you're told.'

The trolley was pushed to the next bed, and the next, and so the busy day wore on. Nurse Elliott spoke no more on the subject to Bob Shaw and her friend Nurse Scott, but it had served to remind Paula that, as she was leaving Hobart the next day, the evening would be her last chance of visiting Bob once more.

So, after handing over to Night Sister, Paula walked along to Allonah Ward. There were the usual little groups of friends and relatives gathered round the various beds, but, as on her previous visit, Bob was alone. Paula started down the ward, and he saw her and waved.

'Thought you were never coming,' he remarked as soon as she was within earshot. 'Sit down where I can see you.' He smiled up into Paula's face. 'You're as beautiful as ever, my sweet.'

She laughed and sat down beside him. 'Well, how are you, Bob?' she asked. 'You're looking very pleased with yourself.'

He grinned and reached for her hand. 'I *am* pleased with myself,' he said, then hesitated and looked away from Paula.

'Come on, tell me,' she urged, and tried to draw away her hand, but his clasp tightened.

'Paula,' he muttered, 'you remember—that night at Wrest Point. You—you said that we were all washed up, you and I. Do you—er—still feel that way?'

Paula looked down at his anxious, worried face, and smiled. 'Yes, Bob, I do,' she said softly. 'And I think that you—' She laughed suddenly. 'Bob, tell me why you're so pleased with yourself—or shall I tell you?'

He looked at her rather like a guilty schoolboy, then grinned sheepishly.

'You're in love, aren't you?' she went on.

'More than that, Paula.' He suddenly gripped the hand he still held. 'I'm—I'm engaged. Please wish me luck.'

She stared at him in amazement, then burst into a delighted laugh. 'Oh, I do, Bob, I do—but that was quick work, wasn't it? Who is she, and—well, go on, tell me everything, right from the beginning.'

Bob laughed and grabbed at Paula's other hand. 'I will if you give me half a chance,' he said protestingly. 'Well, Paula, she's the most wonderful girl in the world. I mean—well—' he grinned shamefacedly, then joined in Paula's laughter, 'after you, of course!'

'Well, go on with the story, Bob,' she said. 'Who is she, and where did you meet her?'

He gave her hand an excited squeeze. 'Right here, Paula,' he whispered. 'She's a nurse in this ward. Her name's Linda Scott. Do you know her?'

'No.' Paula shook her head. 'But I think I've seen her, Bob. She's very pretty.' She laughed. 'But how did you manage to propose—in here?'

He grinned at her. 'It was a bit tricky,' he said, 'but—well, she's on night duty, you see. She used to sit and talk to me, and then—well—' He laughed. 'Are you surprised, Paula?'

She smiled down at his rather embarrassed face. 'Well, Bob, I don't know,' she said. 'But in any case, I'm terribly pleased for you. I really am. She looks a sweet girl. Now, tell me what you plan to do when you leave here. Are you going back to sea or—' and for the next quarter of an hour Paula sat and listened to Bob's happy and excited plans for the future. As she stood up to go he said,

'We're going to get married just as soon as I'm fit again. Linda's parents know, and have been to see me. You'll come to the wedding, won't you, Paula?'

'Of course I will,' she replied. 'Goodbye for now, and—bless you, Bob.'

She walked away feeling very much cheered at the spectacle of Bob's happiness. His affairs are settled, anyway, she thought, and—Christopher's? Well, it rather looks like it, she had to admit. If only things had gone right that first night in this country, then perhaps—but what was the use of all these "ifs"? Paula thought. They'd gone wrong, and had gone on going wrong till now it was too late to do anything about it. Another girl had seized her opportunity, and she, Paula, had lost.

As she entered the club her thoughts turned to Angus. She had not seen much of him since the return from Triabunna, and now she realised that she had missed his cheerful company.

Club Sister came from her office as Paula passed the door. 'Oh, Miss Bruce,' she called, 'there was a telephone message for you—from a Mr Lowther. He said he'd ring again.'

Paula laughed. 'I was thinking of him as I came in,' she said. 'Thank you, Miss North.' She started up the stairs just as the telephone rang again.

'Yes, it's for you,' Sister North said, and handed the receiver to Paula.

'Hello, Angus. Paula here.' She waited for him to reply.

'Ah, got you this time,' he said. 'I believe—er—Rosalind told me that you are returning to Dover tomorrow. Well, my dear, I have to be in tomorrow on business. If you like, I could run you back instead of the coach. What about it?'

Paula hesitated just for a second, then,

'Thank you, Angus,' she said. 'That would be marvellous. Will you call for me at the Club? The time? Oh, as early as you like. Actually, I've finished now, so any time that suits you will be all right for me. Ten? Yes, that'll be lovely. How are you? A party! Are you celebrating something, then? The Apple Festival? Oh, of course, I'd forgotten about that. Well, it depends on the patients, doesn't it? When is it? Well, we'll just have to keep our fingers crossed till next week. Yes, I hope so, too. Good-bye, Angus—till tomorrow.'

Paula continued her way upstairs. Her week in Hobart was now over. The two Sisters from Melbourne had arrived; the Sister who had gone down with fever was now recovered, and so the state of emergency was over. On the whole she had enjoyed working in a big busy hospital again; also it had been the happy ending to the problem of Bob Shaw. But now Paula was ready to return to Dover, and suddenly she hoped fervently that she would not see Christopher again. She must just put him out of her life and hope that Doreen would bring him the happiness he had lost five years ago.

Firmly Paula turned her thoughts to Angus. His face, with its bold angular features and his thick iron-grey hair, came before her. Very attractive, she thought—but not for me. For suddenly, and without a doubt, Paula knew that it had to be Christopher or no one. Though it won't be like that for always, she assured herself. I shall forget him—in time.

The journey back to Dover along the now familiar road was pleasant and enlivening with Angus as a companion.

'I've missed you, apple-blossom,' he said to Paula, 'and I'm sure Rosalind has too. I saw her down on the beach yesterday with young Freeman. She's a fine swimmer.'

'Sounds as if there's not much doing at the hospital,' Paula remarked. 'I must try and get a swim in while the weather is so lovely.' A silence descended upon them, and Paula wondered uneasily if Angus had something on his mind. She began to chatter about her week in Hobart, and was glad when they came within sight of Dover and then the hospital.

Rosalind greeted Paula gaily when she came into the hall, followed by Angus. Rosalind herself was looking particularly attractive. Her fair skin was burnt to a smooth golden brown and her curly hair was now almost ash blonde. The three stood for a few moments in the tiny hall. Angus was talking once more about his idea for an Apple Festival party when the telephone rang. Rosalind went to answer it.

'Yes?' she said, then, 'Oh, hello, Philip, how are you? Yes, fine. What? Apple Festival?' She laughed and glanced back at Paula. 'I don't know. I'll ring you back, shall I? What? Why, yes, I'd love it, of course. It's just that it may not be possible. Yes, I will. Goodbye.' She put down the receiver. 'That was Philip Freeman,' she said over her shoulder. 'He also has ideas about an Apple Festival party.'

Paula hesitated, then looked at Angus. 'Well, why not make it one party?' she suggested brightly, and before Rosalind could reply, Angus said,

'Good idea, Paula. We'll do that, if it's all right with you, Rosalind.' He looked at her and she nodded briefly. 'Well, I must go now.' His voice was abrupt. 'And I'll see you both later on. So don't forget. Apple Festival party is on. Goodbye, girls.'

'I think it will be rather fun, Ross, don't you?' Paula

asked rather tentatively, as she started along the passage towards her room.

Rosalind followed. 'Where's Betty?' Paula asked.

'Yes, I think so too. Betty? Oh, she's having tea with the Renwicks.' Rosalind's voice was very uninterested, Paula thought. Perhaps she'd wanted to go alone with Philip to the Festival.

'Of course we'll have to see what the patient situation is next week,' she said, watching Rosalind's face.

'Susan Renwick has offered to stand in if necessary.' Rosalind stood by the door and watched Paula unlock her case. 'There's only one patient in at present. Jim Foley—the kidney case, you know. He'll be in for a few more days. Did you have a good time at Hobart?'

'A busy time,' Paula said, taking some overalls from the case. 'But yes, I enjoyed it.' She laughed suddenly and looked up into Rosalind's waiting face. 'I saw Bob and—what do you think, Ross?' Her eyes were glinting with merriment, and Rosalind looked at her uncertainly.

'Well,' she said, crossing over to the dressing table, 'what happened?'

Paula began to laugh. 'You'll never guess,' she said, 'but Bob's in love again.' And, sitting back on her heels, Paula told Rosalind all about the romance between him and Nurse Linda Scott.

'Well, I'm—' Rosalind began, then joined in Paula's laughter. But after a few minutes she stopped and just looked at her companion.

'Of course I'm delighted about it all,' Paula said at last, watching Rosalind with puzzled eyes. 'It's a load off my mind.'

'Paula—' Rosalind's voice was abrupt, 'did you see anything of Christopher Deane?'

Paula looked down at her hands and saw with surprise that they were trembling slightly. 'No,' she said, then, after a slight pause, 'and I've given up thinking of him, Ross. What's the use of sighing for something one can't have?'

Rosalind looked at her down-bent head. 'No,' she said

quietly, 'I suppose it is a waste of time. Well—' she shrugged her shoulders and took a step towards the door, 'I must go and see how our one and only patient is faring. Then I'll telephone Philip. We shall be quite a big party for the Apple Festival.'

'Four's not so big,' Paula remarked, shutting the suitcase with a bang. She was conscious again of that intangible barrier between herself and her friend. I wish she'd tell me about Philip Freeman, Paula thought, but she never tells me anything these days.

'Six,' Rosalind said calmly, strolling to the door. 'Angus, you and I, Philip and his girl and, I think, Tim Halloran.'

Paula got slowly to her feet. She stared at Rosalind for a full minute, then said, 'Did you say—*Philip's* girl friend?'

'Yes,' Rosalind replied. She looked round at Paula. 'Didn't you know? But then you've been away such a lot, haven't you? Or I have. Yes, she's doing her nursing training in Melbourne. She and Phil have known each other since schooldays, and now they've just got engaged. She's over here on holiday. I haven't met her yet, but she's coming to the party next week. I'd better get cracking. See you at tea-time.'

CHAPTER FOURTEEN

AFTER Rosalind had gone Paula stood for a few minutes staring out of the window. The sea glittered under the hot afternoon sun, and idly she watched a girl in a yellow swimsuit preparing to dive from the float. She was still not quite recovered from the surprise, almost shock of Rosalind's words. Had the news of Philip's engagement been a shock to her too? And yet, Paula thought, she'd got the clear impression that it was no news to Rosalind; that she'd known all along. Then why had she never mentioned it? Was Rosalind merely trying to save her own face? Paula wondered unhappily; and hoped not. Slowly she turned away from the window. There's nothing I can do about it, she thought, not with this—barrier between us.

Paula walked into the kitchen where she found Minnie stuffing a chicken, with Betty Anderson watching her and drinking a cup of tea. 'Hello, Paula,' she said, and went to the cupboard for another cup. 'I'm getting a bit tired of being on a special diet,' she added, looking at the chicken on the table. 'All Jim Foley's fault, too. The report was positive, did you know?'

'Yes, Ross told me.' Paula looked at Minnie's preparations and smiled. 'That's the drawback of one patient,' she said. 'And if he happens to be on a special diet, then it's special diet for the staff, too. Sorry, Betty, but I like chicken.'

'One can have too much of a good thing. Are you going to the Apple Festival party?'

'If it's at all possible,' Paula replied, 'but not if I'm needed here.'

'Quite a party, isn't it? It'll be nice to see Hilda James again.'

'Hilda—' Paula said questioningly, 'is that—'

'Philip Freeman's girl friend? Yes. I knew her in Melbourne. She's a nice kid, too. Maybe too good for him.'

So that's it, Paula thought. That explains the strained relations between Betty and Rosalind. Betty had thought that Rosalind was setting her cap at Philip, whereas it did seem that Rosalind had known all along about the other girl. Or had she? Paula shrugged her shoulders and poured herself a cup of tea. Ross told her nothing these days. She could only hope that some day the reason for it all would be made clear.

On the day of the party a second patient came in—a maternity case. Dr Renwick had diagnosed twins some time ago and had told the patient to come into hospital in good time as twins were often early. After examining Mrs Drew he told Betty and Paula that he did not think the babies would arrive for another week at least. 'But we'll keep her in, of course,' he said, 'just in case. Oh, and there's no need for anyone to stay away from the Apple Festival,' he added, smiling at Rosalind's anxious face. 'Susan is waiting to come in whenever you want her. We shall both be here.'

'I'm not going to the party,' Betty pointed out. 'I wasn't invited.'

There was a slightly uncomfortable silence.

'Oh, in that case, then,' Dr Renwick hastened to add, 'there will be plenty of us here on the spot.'

After dinner Paula and Rosalind went to their rooms to change from their white overalls to gay summer frocks. And presently Paula heard the sound of a car coming up the drive. She heard Rosalind leave her room, and then several voices laughing and talking in the hall.

Paula followed Rosalind, and was in time to see her shaking hands with a slim, dark-haired girl of about twenty. Paula was then introduced to Hilda, who seemed to be a bright, friendly type of girl. Betty joined them just as Angus arrived in his Holden Special.

'Hello, there,' he called as he ran up the steps and into the little hall. 'Everyone set for the party?'

'Come and meet Hilda, Mr Lowther,' Philip said with obvious pride, and drawing his girl forward. 'We've just got engaged.'

Paula happened to be watching Angus's face at that moment. She saw his eyes move quickly to Rosalind's face, and something in his expression suddenly told her the truth. She stared at him in amazement, but he was now smiling and talking to Hilda. Did I really see him looking at Rosalind like that? Paula wondered, feeling quite dazed for the moment. Perhaps it was just that he was feeling sorry for her. But no, she was sure it wasn't that. It was love she had seen in Angus's eyes. He was in love with Rosalind—probably had been right from the first. And suddenly Paula wanted to laugh. It rose in her throat uncontrollably; and muttering some excuse, she turned and rushed along to her room.

Arrived there, Paula subsided on to her bed, giggling helplessly. First Christopher, she thought, then Bob, and now Angus. Well, well, perhaps fate means me to dedicate myself to my profession, and end up as a dignified, well-upholstered Matron of a training hospital. Yes, she thought, giggling again, that's probably it.

When Paula rejoined the rest of the party she looked around for Rosalind. For it had occurred to her that the latter was still an unknown quantity. The fact that Angus was in love with her did not necessarily mean that it was the same with Rosalind. But Paula saw that she was already sitting beside Tim Halloran at the wheel of his car.

'Come along, Paula,' Angus called. 'I've been waiting for you. Are you ready?'

'Sure it's all right for both of us to go?' Paula asked Frank Renwick, who was standing beside Betty and waiting to see everyone off.'

He patted her shoulder. 'Of course,' he said. 'In any case you'll both be back this evening. Be off and enjoy yourselves.'

Paula followed Angus down the steps; the other car

had already moved off. She stole a side-glance at her companion as he got in beside her and saw that he was looking very thoughtful.

'What time does it start, Angus?' Paula asked.

'Well, the actual show starts at two-thirty in the Recreation Ground at Cygnet. You know, the procession the crowning of the Apple Queen, and all that nonsense. Then, in the evening, there's the usual thing. Dancing on the green, and a barbecue.' He paused, then said, 'We pass through Franklin before we get to Cygnet. That's where Rosalind went for a short time, wasn't it? Er—how is she taking this?'

'Taking what?' Paula asked, knowing full well what Angus meant.

His face flushed and he looked away from her. 'This engagement business,' he muttered. 'I thought that—'

'Oh, you mean—Philip Freeman and Rosalind?' Paula laughed. 'Well, apparently she's known about Hilda all along. It's been just a beautiful friendship, Angus.'

He said nothing, just stared in front of him, and Paula also relapsed into silence. There's nothing I can do, she thought. I don't know how Rosalind feels, so I must be careful not to give him any false hopes, but I'm beginning to wonder if this explains her attitude to me. Oh, I do hope so. For a brief moment Paula's thoughts turned to Christopher and his farewell kiss, then resolutely she set herself to forget him and enjoy the party.

'There's Cygnet,' Angus said, rousing himself to talk to her. The road was now following the winding course of the River Huon. Paula looked to where he was pointing, just across the river.

'Oh, we're nearly there,' she observed in surprise, but he shook his head.

' 'Fraid not,' he said. 'We have to cross the river, and there's no bridge till we get to Franklin, and that's some miles on. Over there,' he waved an arm, 'is the old wooden bridge, but it's not safe to use now. You'll see the fine new stone one when we get round the bend.

Paula,' he stopped for a moment, then went on talking in a jerky kind of voice, 'would you say that it would be fair for me to ask a girl—a young girl, only half my age—to—er—marry me? I mean—' he hesitated, then jerked on, 'my heart, you know, and—well, d'you think—?' He suddenly turned and looked at her from anxious eyes.

Paula looked away. For one dreadful moment she wanted to laugh as she recalled a similar scene at lunch in the Wrest Point Hotel on the way back from Triabunna. She had thought then— With a great effort she turned to Angus and smiled into his waiting face.

'I think you worry too much about your heart condition,' she said. 'You only need to take reasonable care. And as for the—other point, I don't think forty-seven is such a terrible age—not in these days when heaps of people live to be nearly a hundred. Anyway, why don't—' Paula stopped. She had been about to add, 'Why don't you ask her?' but changed her mind. She still had no idea how Rosalind felt. No, Angus must manage this for himself, and I hope he's more successful than I've been, Paula concluded rather bleakly.

Angus nodded his head thoughtfully, then returned her smile. 'Thanks, my dear,' he said. 'I'll think it over, but I'm glad you don't think I'm an old man. Yes,' he nodded his head again, 'I'll—certainly think it over.'

Paula laughed. 'Don't take too long over the thinking,' she advised, then added teasingly, 'After all, you're not getting any younger.'

He laughed heartily, but somewhat to Paula's disappointment, dropped the subject.

When they reached the festival grounds at Cygnet, everything was in full swing. There were side shows and stalls with pyramids of polished apples as well as other fruit. Women and girls in gay summer frocks and young men in white shorts and shirts were strolling about and commenting loudly on the various exhibits. The procession was just about to start as Paula and Angus joined the other four. A stream of decorated drays, each with its attendant, trundled past them, and loud laughing voices drew attention to the goods they advertised.

'Here comes the Apple Queen,' Philip said. 'We'll get a good view of the robing and crowning ceremony from here.' He was standing with one arm thrown over Hilda's shoulders and the other linked through Rosalind's arm. Paula saw from the corner of her eye that Angus had moved purposefully up on the other side. She smiled to herself.

'You'd have made a lovely Apple Queen, Paula.' It was Tim Halloran speaking, and he had moved up to her side. 'Look, just your colour.'

Paula looked. The crimson satin robe was being slipped over the young girl's shoulders, then, amid loud "Ohs" of admiration from the watching crowd, the glittering crown of gold tinsel was placed upon her head.

'Paula, come and watch the competition for the apple grading and packing,' Tim suggested, taking her arm and drawing her a few paces away from the rest of the party. Paula gave a quick glance and saw that Angus had succeeded in detaching Rosalind from Philip and was drawing her away towards the edge of the crowd. Good luck to him, Paula thought as she allowed herself to be led away by Tim. 'Here it is,' he said. Paula watched with fascinated eyes as a row of young men sorted the piles of fruit with lightning-like rapidity according to size, colour and quality.

'I'm quite dizzy watching them,' she laughed. 'It's quite uncanny.'

'Yes, they're good,' Tim said. 'Like to see the log-chopping competition? It's over here.' He led her on and over to the side of the arena. Paula saw several flat sawn-off tree-trunks about a couple of feet high. Across them were laid logs about a foot and a half in diameter. Beside each stood a brawny youth stripped to the waist and carrying a chopper. 'They're due to start any minute now,' Tim said.

While they waited Paula looked about her with lively interest. The Festival ground was a bright emerald green, mown to the smoothness of velvet. It was a natural clearing set in a frame of tall grey-green euca-lyptus trees. She could see clusters of light bulbs among the leaves. All around were the tall pyramids of crimson, green and yellow apples looking themselves like coloured lights. There was a band playing at one end of the ground, and in a second and smaller clearing at one side Paula could see the preparations for a barbecue were going on.

'They're starting,' Tim said suddenly, and squeezing her arm to attract her attention. Paula turned her atten-tion to the brawny young competitors. 'Now watch,' he said tensely, and at the same moment the choppers were swung in the air, then down on to the logs. Paula gasped as wood chippings began to fly in every direction. The gleaming axes made swift and incredible arcs through the air, and the pace was so terrific that it was difficult to see who was wielding them. The tough logs disappeared like melting snow.

'Heavens!' Paula said, clutching Tim's arm as the crowd behind suddenly pushed them forward. '*How* do they keep up such a speed? It's—' She stopped and her heart quickened its beat. Just opposite herself and Tim, she had seen another couple, the girl also clinging to the man's arm. Christopher and Doreen. The crowd moved and hid them, but even in the momentary glimpse she had had, Paula knew that Christopher had seen her.

At that moment all the lights were switched on, and for an instant the effect was quite dazzling. The whole arena became a blaze of light and colour. The only spectacle the dazed Paula could liken it to, and which she had seen once, was the Blackpool illuminations. She gazed round her, blinking. All the side stalls, cafés and tents were suddenly things of fairy-like beauty, and the car of the Apple Queen, which was slowly completing the course, was like something out of Hans Andersen. The barbecue sprang to life, and from it came the delicious scents of roasting meats, chicken, steaks and sausages.

Paula became aware of a sudden quiet. The log-chopping competition was over. There was a burst of cheering; but among the medley of bright, twinkling lights, laughing voices, rousing music from the band, and a hundred and one other sounds and sights Paula hadn't an idea as to who was the winner.

'Did you bring a coat with you?' Tim asked, then laughed as Paula swung her yellow cardigan into view. 'Shows how observant I am, but it gets chilly later on. Where would you like to go now? How about a drink?'

'Jolly good idea,' Paula said. 'All this noise and excitement has given me a beautiful thirst. Oh, look, Tim, there are the others,' and she waved an arm towards the advancing figures of the rest of the party. I mustn't think of Christopher, she kept saying to herself, I *won't* think of him.

'Hello, you two,' Angus said, joining them. 'Who says a schooner?' He had an arm round Rosalind's shoulders, and her eyes were very bright. Paula looked quickly at Rosalind's laughing face, but could learn nothing from it. Philip and Hilda came up then, and Angus led the way into one of the tents.

'Schooner for you, Paula?' he asked. 'And where have you been? I looked for you everywhere.'

'Sure?' she asked, smiling and taking the tall glass he handed to her. Angus grinned in reply. He's looking quite excited, Paula thought. I wonder—

After they had all quenched their thirst Philip suggested a visit to the barbecue. 'I'm hungry,' he said. 'Come on, Hilda.' He tucked her hand in his arm. 'Where's Ross?'

'Don't be greedy, young feller,' Angus said, putting an arm round Rosalind's waist. 'I'm looking after her—and Paula,' and he slipped the other arm round her. Tim brought up the rear.

'What a gorgeous fire!' Paula said a minute later as they watched the huge grill and spit cooking the food. The three men, with Hilda, went off to collect the food while she and Rosalind sat on the grass to wait for them.

'Enjoying it, Ross?' Paula asked, watching her companion's face.

'Yes, rather. Are you?' Their eyes met, and Paula waited. 'Paula—' Rosalind began, then stopped and looked towards the barbecue. 'Here are the others,' she said. 'Haven't been long, have they?'

'Come along, girls,' Angus called as he drew near, 'make ready for the feast. Here we are. What was yours, Paula? Catch!' and he pretended to throw the steak into her lap. Paula noticed with satisfaction that he sat down very close to Rosalind.

'These sausages are good,' Philip remarked a few minutes later. 'Anyone for any more?'

'How's the steak, Paula, my love?' Tim asked, shuffling nearer to her and bringing his face very close to hers.

'Oh, Tim,' Paula said, laughing, but drawing back from him, 'your face is all greasy. Go away!' There was a light-hearted scuffle between the pair, and while it was going on Angus, who had been looking over their shoulders, suddenly exclaimed, 'I say, folk's there's Chris Deane over there.'

Tim, who was beginning to look annoyed with Paula, turned at once and said eagerly, '*And* the charming redhead.' He paused, then added, 'They're coming this way, too.'

Paula straightened up and put a hand to her hair.

'Hello, folks.' It was his voice.

'Hello, there Chris,' Angus said, looking up. 'Sit down and join us.'

'Thanks,' Christopher said. 'Hello, Paula.' She looked up at him. 'Enjoying yourself?' He nodded to the rest of the group, then turned to the girl beside him. 'Doreen, have you met—'

'Yes, of course.' The girl's voice was impatient, even rude. 'Oh, come on, Chris, I want something from the barbecue. I'm—'

'Allow me,' Tim said. He had been watching the girl

with unconcealed admiration, and now he scrambled eagerly to his feet. She looked at him in surprise, then a slow smile spread across her face.

'All right,' she said, dropping Christopher's arm, and moving towards the other man. 'Lead me to it.'

'Sit down,' Angus said again to Christopher as the two disappeared in the crowd. 'Ross and I are just going to take these plates back, and then we'll rejoin you.' He got up and drew Rosalind to her feet; and then Paula saw with quickened breath that Philip and Hilda had already slipped quietly away. She and Christopher were alone together.

He looked down at her for a moment, then said abruptly, 'Your escort seems to have deserted you.'

Paula felt her lips tighten. 'Yes, doesn't he?' she returned lightly. 'Perhaps he prefers red hair to black. Anyway, he's not my particular escort.' Her hand went again to her ruffled hair.

'No,' Christopher said. 'I believe you.'

Paula got to her feet. She felt at a disadvantage sitting there on the grass with him towering over her.

'I just don't understand you at all,' he went on, looking down at his feet. 'Why do you make yourself so—' He stopped as Paula's head jerked up and she stared at him in amazement. What had he been going to say? What did he mean?

'So—what?' she asked, colour flaring in her cheeks. 'What were you going to say?' She stood stiffly in front of him, and Christopher moved restlessly.

'Look here, do you mind if we walk a little way?' he asked. 'Perhaps I shouldn't have said—well,' he took Paula by the elbow and drew her on with him. She glanced at him and saw that his face was red under the tan. 'Your eyes, Paula,' his voice was low and sounded angry, 'they're so clear—and true. You look so sweet, and—and yet—'

'Yes, what?' Incredulous indignation was in her voice. 'I—don't understand you.' She looked sideways at him, then added, 'And I've almost given up trying.'

'Yes, I'm sure you have. Why should you, anyway?' He stopped abruptly, and twisted her round to face him. 'Paula, why do you *do* it?' he asked roughly. 'Especially now?'

She stared at him in puzzled anger, yet with excitement rising in her. 'But—do what?' she asked.

His grey eyes stared down into hers. 'All these men friends that you're on such affectionate terms with,' he muttered. 'Four at least in that many months.' He stopped speaking, and Paula saw a muscle twitching at the corner of his mouth. 'I—thought at one time—'

'But—but,' she broke in, and then her temper got the better of her. 'The friends I make are my own business,' Paula said. 'You're nothing but a nasty, suspicious, narrow-minded—' She stopped suddenly and looked away from Christopher's face. There was a look in his eyes that made her feel mean and uncomfortable, and she remembered all at once the story that Miss Needham had told her. The tragedy that lay only five years back in this man's life. She shifted uneasily. Then something he had just said made Paula turn on him again. What was it he'd said? Yes: 'Especially now.' What exactly did he mean?

She looked again into Christopher's flushed face. 'But what is it to you?' she asked him more quietly, 'and why should *you* disapprove? And why do you say "especially now"? I'd like to know what all this is about.' Paula's voice was controlled now, but beneath the mixed feelings of anger, resentment, and surprise, the hidden excitement was again rising in her. She had asked him, 'What is it to you?' and now, with quickened breathing, she waited for his answer. There was silence for a few moments, then Christopher dropped the arm he was still holding and half-turned away.

'Paula,' he said in a low voice, 'I'm sorry if I've offended you. I shouldn't have spoken as I did. It's no business of mine, I know, but—' he turned again to face her, 'do you think it's quite fair?'

She stared at him speechlessly for a moment. 'Fair!'

she echoed at last, genuinely puzzled—and disappointed. 'Fair to whom, or what?'

Christopher suddenly took her by the shoulders, and
shook her. 'To him, of course,' he said roughly. 'To that
poor devil in hospital in Hobart. How do you think he
would feel if he'd seen you as I did just now—cuddling
up to that fellow Halloran, and him kissing you?'

Paula stared at him open-mouthed, too surprised even
to resent his rough handling of her. 'And it was only
yesterday,' Christopher continued, 'that you and Shaw
became engaged. Have you forgotten already, or
doesn't it mean anything to you?'

CHAPTER FIFTEEN

PAULA walked into the bathroom and started to scrub up just in case she was needed in the labour ward. Mrs Drew was in there, and the twins would be making their appearance in the world at any moment now. Rosalind was with her. Another patient, an accident case from a nearby farm, had come in about half an hour ago, and Dr Renwick and Sister Anderson were attending to him. Paula was officially off duty, but she was too unsettled in her mind to think of resting.

She finished scrubbing her nails and started back for the labour ward. She was still dazed from the incident of the previous night. When Christopher had spoken those incredible words, she had at first stared at him, then started to laugh. It was half hysterical, and though, at the sight of his face, she had tried to stop, it had kept bubbling up. The whole situation now began to seem ridiculous to Paula. How had Christopher come to make such a mistake?

And then the explanation, such a simple one, too, had come to her. Christopher had seen her on that first visit to Bob, had seen them holding hands, and probably heard Bob say something about giving him a kiss. And then Paula could almost see what had happened. Christopher had visited Bob just after her next visit when he had told her about Linda Scott. And almost certainly he had told Christopher that he had just become engaged, to a nurse, who was the most beautiful girl, etc., etc. And then there was the incident of her meeting with Christopher just after seeing Mrs Griffiths, when she'd been feeling so happy for her. No doubt he'd connected that happiness with Bob and his recovery from the operation. Paula sighed heavily. Was there to be no end to all these misunderstandings?

And it was while she was trying to get her ill-timed mirth under control that she had heard a shout, and there were Angus and Rosalind hurrying towards them. Rosalind was laughing and waving to Paula.

'Hurry up!' she called. 'It's time we were getting back. We told Doc—' and Paula suddenly stopped laughing and looked at Christopher's angry, bewildered face. I mustn't leave it like this, she thought frantically, I must— 'But, Chris,' she gabbled, catching her breath on the words, 'you've got it all wrong about me—and Bob. We're not engaged. *He* is, but it's another girl. He told me all about it. I'm not—you—' but it was too late. Rosalind and Angus were there, standing right in front of her, and telling her to hurry; and she'd had to go.

Paula had a vague recollection of Angus bringing herself and Rosalind back, and Christopher, with frustrated looks, disappearing in search of Doreen. Paula's two companions had been very quiet on the return journey, but it was not the silence of constraint, and Paula felt that something had happened between them. She wondered if Rosalind would confide in her after Angus had gone. But on reaching the hospital, there had been no opportunity for talk. Paula had taken over from Betty, who was with Mrs Drew, and now this morning Rosalind was there.

As she walked back along the corridor, the thought uppermost in Paula's mind was—would Christopher get in touch with her today? Surely he would, Paula thought, but—and here her heart sank—there was the girl, Doreen. What part did she play, or was about to play, in his life? Was it true that they were to marry? Paula's perplexed thoughts made the idea of sleep impossible.

Rosalind's eyes looked at her in surprise from above the mask, then she smiled. 'Keep on with the gas and air, Mrs Drew,' she said to the woman on the bed, 'you're doing very well.'

Paula came and stood on the other side. 'The cots and blankets are ready,' she said to Rosalind in a low voice, then turned at a slight sound to see Dr Renwick at the door. He beckoned her outside.

'I want you to go along to the other ward,' he said. 'Betty's not feeling too good this morning. The patient has been attended to, and I think he'll come good. I've fixed up the gash in his thigh, and he's just had a quarter of morphine. But he's suffering badly from shock, Paula, and I want you to stay with him. How is she?' and he nodded towards the labour ward.

'Well, she's fully dilated,' Paula replied, 'and coming on quite quickly. The first looks like being a big child, but I don't think it will be too difficult. She's being very co-operative.'

He nodded his head. 'Right. I'll have a look at her right away. You trot along now.'

At midday, Rosalind handed over to Betty, who was now quite recovered. The twins, weighing ten pounds between them, were lying snugly in two blue-draped cots—they were both boys. Jim Foley, his foot almost well, was preparing to go out the following morning, and the latest accident case was now sleeping peacefully. Paula had already gone to her room to rest when there was a knock at the door. Her heart leapt to her throat. Was it—would it be a message from him? Oh, surely there was time for him to have telephoned her. 'Come in,' she called faintly, and Rosalind's head came from round the door.

'Oh, hello,' she said, and hesitated. 'Am I keeping you up?' Paula saw that she was carrying a tray with two cups of tea.

'No, of course not,' she said, smiling her welcome. 'I'm not a bit sleepy, and I'd love a cuppa. Come in.'

'I've had a letter from Daddy,' Rosalind said, looking slightly flushed. She came and sat beside Paula on the bed. 'It's a telling-off letter, for both of us. He says they haven't had a letter from either of us for two weeks, and they're getting worried.'

Paula took a cup from the tray. 'Oh, dear!' she said. 'I forgot last week, but I'll write this very day. We both will, eh?' She looked at Rosalind and the two smiled at each other. Miraculously, the barrier between them had melted away, and the old familiar Ross was back. Paula waited, wondering if some interesting and exciting news was forthcoming, but Rosalind continued prosaically enough.

'Yes, I'll write to them both,' she said. 'Good do yesterday, wasn't it, Paula?' She hesitated. 'I had a letter from Miss Needham this morning. There's one for you, too.' She took it from her overall pocket and handed it to Paula. 'It's about a place called King Island. She wonders if we'd like to do a tour there together, and says she spoke to you about it.'

Paula opened the letter, read it, then looked at Rosalind. 'Yes, she did,' she replied. 'I was going to ask you, Ross, but—'

'I know what you're going to say, Paula—and I'm sorry. I wanted to explain about that.' Rosalind's face was flushed and she avoided Paula's eye.

'Don't worry.' The ready smile flashed out. 'Well, what about King Island, Ross? I met a Tourist Sister in Hobart who'd done a spell there, and she said it was bonzer. But—' Paula gave a quick side-glance, 'perhaps you have other plans.'

A bright blush rose to Rosalind's cheeks, and she gave a sudden excited little laugh. 'Well, yes, I have,' she said. 'I—I don't think it will be King Island for me, Paula. I think it will be—England.'

Paula stared at her in puzzled dismay. 'England!' she echoed, and Rosalind nodded.

'Oh, Paula,' she squeezed her suddenly round the waist, 'I—I've got something to tell you. Something I never, never thought would happen to me.' She gave Paula another excited squeeze. 'I don't suppose you'll ever guess, but—Angus has asked me to marry him!' She stopped, breathless, then added, 'and we're spending the honeymoon in England.'

'Well!' Paula said, and again, 'well!' and they both started to laugh.

'I knew you'd be surprised,' Rosalind went on, 'but, as a matter of fact, I think I fell in love with Angus when he was here in hospital, but he—oh, it's been misunderstandings all along. He thought I'd fallen for Phil Freeman, but of course that was nothing. I knew about Hilda from the first. Then Angus thought he was too old, *and* he was worried about his heart, and he didn't think it was fair, and well, you know—'

'Oh, Ross dear,' Paula interrupted, and kissed the glowing cheek near her own, 'I can't tell you how pleased I am. Angus is such a dear. I must say you kept it very dark; I thought it was Philip, too. I'm so glad, and I'm sure you'll be very happy.'

'We will. I'm absolutely thrilled now,' Rosalind said, and paused. 'D'you know, Paula,' she added sheepishly, 'I thought Angus was in love with you.'

So did I for a while, Paula thought. She smiled at Rosalind and said, 'What a ridiculous idea!'

'Oh, Paula, it'll be wonderful seeing Mummy and Daddy again so soon.' She stopped and Paula looked at her questioningly. 'Paula,' she said again, her face serious all at once, 'I'm sorry I've been such a—a pig lately. I—I was jealous, you know. I thought, almost from the first, that Angus had fallen for you. It got worse and worse, and—' she looked really unhappy now, 'I even got to hoping that you and Bob would make it up again so that—oh, Paula, do forgive me for being such a selfish beast.'

Paula put an impulsive arm round her shoulders. 'You're not,' she said, giving her a little shake. 'Forget it, Ross. Be happy, and don't worry about anything any more. Everything's just as it used to be.'

Rosalind gave her a grateful smile. 'But, Paula,' she said presently, 'what about—Christopher? Is he really engaged to that girl? I hoped when I saw you and him together last night that—' There was a knock at the door and Minnie half entered.

'Telephone for Sister Lane,' she said, and vanished.

Rosalind jumped to her feet. 'That'll be Angus,'

she said. 'I'll leave you to your bed, Paula. See you later.'

Paula yawned widely and lay back on the pillows. She supposed she might as well get some sleep if possible, and she was tired of thinking and wondering about Christopher. It's up to him now, Paula thought, and closed her eyes.

When she awoke, Paula saw by the rays of the sun streaming in at her window that it was evening. She had slept for nearly six hours, and as she sat up in bed a thought, a question, slid into her mind. Christopher! Had there been a message from him? After a moment Paula rose and went to the washbasin. She was just buttoning herself into a clean white overall when Rosalind quietly opened the door, then came in.

'Oh, so you're awake at last,' she said, then added, 'take off that overall, Paula. Everything's quiet, and Betty and I are coping. No need for three of us to be jostling each other. Why don't you go out for a breath of air after supper? It's a gorgeous evening.'

Paula walked slowly over to the window and looked out. 'Yes,' she said, 'it's an idea,' and she started to unbutton the overall. 'I'll go for a walk along the beach.' She was feeling quite sick with disappointment. She knew, without asking, that there was no message for her. Rosalind would have made it her business to find out before coming to her room. 'It *is* a lovely evening,' she said to Rosalind, trying to sound eager and lighthearted. 'How is Angus?'

'Fine.' Rosalind smiled and blushed as she met Paula's eye. 'He's coming round this evening. Betty says we can have the sitting room.' She laughed and added, 'Betty's got quite fond of me since she found out that I wasn't trying to steal Philip from her pal Hilda. Which way will you go, Paula?'

'Along by the overhanging gardens, I think,' Paula replied, doing her best to look enthusiastic. 'It's quiet that way. How do I look?' She had slipped a red and yellow striped sleeveless frock over her head, and was

standing in front of the mirror. Rosalind gave a low
wolf-whistle.

'Smashing,' she said. 'You're lucky to be able to wear
those violent colours. They'd make me look like a
ghost.'

At the supper table Paula was careful to ask Betty if
she could be spared before setting out for her walk.
After all, she thought, Betty *is* in charge of the hospital.
Sam, the gardener, was pottering about among the
flower beds as Paula came down the steps. She exchanged greetings with him, and he stood for a moment
watching the red and yellow frock as she crossed the
road and went down on to the beach. There were few
people about as it was getting late, but the air was still
warm and balmy.

Paula strolled along in the direction of what she and
Rosalind called the overhanging gardens. They belonged to some beach houses and stretched right down
to the low jutting bank which separated the beach from
the road. As she approached these gardens Paula could
smell the sweet scent of the boronia bushes which
bordered the lower edges of the gardens. There was a
flat, comfortable-looking rock in her path, so, spreading
wide her red and yellow skirt, Paula sat down and gazed
idly out to sea.

The red ball of sun was on the point of slipping over
the edge of the horizon, and even as she watched, it sank,
leaving behind it the rose-stained glow of sunset sky.
Two or three fishing boats bobbed on the water at the
end of the jetty, and Paula's nostrils caught the fishy
smell of the nets. Tiny wavelets crept up the ribbed
beach, then broke with a soft little smack on the pale
sand. From a clump of eucalyptus just behind her came
the drowsy, almost inaudible chatter of a magpie. The
sweet-scented boronia was now struggling for pre-
cedence with the heavy bitter-almond perfume of pink
oleanders, and Paula thought she could also detect a
faint hint of the delicate red flower of the hibiscus.
She sniffed appreciatively, and thought how much

she loved this beautiful country.

Sliding on to the warm sand with her back to the rock, she gazed dreamily out to sea. Suppose I don't hear anything from Christopher, Paula thought, what then? But before she could find an answer to her own question, a sudden scraping sound behind her made her turn her head. Then, seeing him silhouetted against the slowly-fading sky, she sat quite still, and looked up at him.

'Paula,' Christopher said, his voice very low, and came and stood in front of her, 'I had to see you—to apologise.' He looked down at her, then out to sea.

Paula's hands were clasped tightly in her lap. 'How—how did you know where to find me?' she asked in a jerky, breathless sort of voice. Her heart was racing under the red and yellow striped bodice and she pressed her hands to the excitement that was rising there. Christopher half-smiled, then looked round and selected a rock near Paula's.

'Rosalind told me,' he said. 'Paula,' he stood up again as if unable to rest, 'I'm sorry about last night. I've been wrong about you—all along the line. Will you—' He paused and looked down at her, and she saw the look of entreaty in his eyes.

'It's—all right, Chris,' Paula said softly. 'I understand.'

He scraped a foot on the sand and looked out to sea. 'I wonder if you do,' he said slowly, and turned again to watch her face. 'Last night you called me narrow-minded, suspicious—oh, yes,' he went on as Paula started to protest, 'and you were quite right—I am.'

'No,' Paula said, rising quickly to her feet. 'Please, Chris, I—do understand, really. Don't—say any more.'

He looked into her flushed face, and there was a silence. 'So—you know about—my wife?' he said at last, and Paula nodded.

'Well, that's all over, thank God,' Christopher said abruptly. 'But there are other things.'

What things? Paula wondered, and waited for him to go on.

'I saw Shaw this morning,' Christopher said suddenly, and gave Paula a rather sheepish smile.

'Well, now you know,' she said, and added, 'Bob and I *were* engaged once—a long time ago. He broke it off—and I'm very glad now!'

Christopher moved a step nearer. 'Why?' he asked. The question seemed to hang tensely in the still air. The bitter-sweet scent of the oleanders drifted across to Paula; and ever after she was to connect this scent with herself—and Christopher, standing there on the deserted beach, and looking into each other's eyes. 'Why, Paula?' he asked again, but her courage failed her. She could not tell him, yet, that she loved him.

'Because it would have been a mistake,' Paula answered, and half-turned away from him. She watched the bobbing fishing boats without really seeing them. There's Doreen, she was thinking. I must know about her. Was she one of the "other things" he had mentioned?

Christopher was silent, and Paula sought desperately in her mind for some sort of leading question. She stooped, picked up a pebble, and threw it into the water. He watched its flight.

'When are you—off to the mainland?' Paula asked.

He looked at her, then took a cigarette case from his pocket and flipped it open.

'Smoke?' he asked, holding it out. Paula shook her head.

'In about six weeks,' he added, answering her question.

Paula coughed, hesitated, a moment, then blurted out, 'I—I suppose you'll be getting married over there.'

'Married!' Christopher said, snapping the case shut, and staring at Paula. 'Well—' he spoke slowly, 'perhaps—I—' he came a step nearer. 'What made you ask that question?'

Flaring colour was pulsing uncomfortably in Paula's cheeks, but she had to go on. 'Well, I thought—' she began, then stopped and started again. 'I thought—that you—' She looked at him with parted lips, and he took a swift pace forward.

'Paula,' he said, and put both hands gently on her shoulders. There was silence, except for the tiny slap of the waves and the answering whisper of the sand as it was drawn back with the tide. Paula looked up into Christopher's eyes and waited. Doreen was forgotten; everything was forgotten but herself—and Christopher, here in a world of their own.

'Paula—darling,' he said, his voice a caress, 'I know I'm too old for someone as young and lovely as you—and I have a daughter—and I'm going to a life that won't be easy, especially for a woman, but—' He paused, and Paula trembled beneath the light pressure of his hands. A breeze laden with the fused scents of boronia and oleander lifted the dark hair from her brow, and Christopher raised one hand and smoothed it back. 'Come with me, Paula,' he whispered. 'Marry me.'

'Oh!' The word came from her lips in a long sigh. 'Yes, oh, yes!' and her arms went round his neck. The scented breeze swept across the two tightly-clasped figures and there was silence out there on the beach of Esperance Bay.

Christopher was the first to move. He looked down into the shadowy face raised to his.

'I love you, Paula,' he said. 'From the moment I first saw you.' He bent his face and gently kissed her lips. 'And you—my darling?'

Paula nodded, too dazedly happy to speak. It was true, she was thinking. All the doubts and misunderstandings had melted away. Christopher loved her and she loved him. And she would marry him and go with him wherever he went. 'Come and sit down, darling,' he said, and led her to the rocks. 'Now, when will you marry me? Tomorrow, next week?' He laughed, a laugh of pure happiness. 'Doreen's going to get a surprise,' he added, and laughed again.

Paula was conscious of a slight shock. She had forgotten about Doreen. Now she turned and looked questioningly into his face.

'Chris,' she said, 'who—is Doreen? I mean—' She stopped and he looked at her in surprise.

'Why, she's my cousin,' he said. 'From Melbourne. Over here for a holiday.' He grinned suddenly at Paula, looking surprisingly young and boyish as he did so. 'As a matter of fact, darling, she did have some idea about being my housekeeper, but I told her I didn't need one, especially where I'm going—with you.' He leaned to her on the last words and there was a blissful moment of silence as their lips met.

'When does she go back, Chris?' Paula asked, raising her head from his shoulder.

He laughed. 'I wouldn't be surprised if she doesn't,' he said. 'D'you know, darling, she and Halloran seem to have taken a great fancy to each other. She had lunch with him today, and is having dinner with him this evening. And she tells me—oh, darling, let's talk about us— not Doreen. *We* are much more interesting, don't you think?' He turned Paula's face up to his and traced the curve of one eyebrow with a gentle finger. 'So beautiful!' he murmured. 'Paula—say it.' And her sigh of happiness seemed one with the sweet scents of the night.

'I love you, Chris,' Paula said. 'I love you.'

Two more Doctor Nurse Romances to look out for this month

Mills & Boon Doctor Nurse Romances are proving very popular indeed. Stories range wide throughout the world of medicine – from high-technology modern hospitals to the lonely life of a nurse in a small rural community.

These are the other two titles for February.

THE NEW PUPIL MIDWIFE
by Lisa Cooper

From the moment pupil-midwife Sally Ashford encounters Matthew Tregonna, senior registrar at the Princess Beatrice Hospital, sparks fly. So how could she possibly fall in love with Matthew when she doesn't even like him?

STAFF NURSE AT ST HELEN'S
by Clare Lavenham

When Nurse Melanie Lister leaves home to share a flat she is disturbed to find that Andrew Forbes, a new house surgeon, is to be one of her flatmates. She is determined to dislike him, so why is she so concerned when he falls gravely ill?

On sale where you buy Mills & Boon romances

The Mills & Boon rose is the rose of romance

Look out for these three great Doctor Nurse Romances coming next month

HOSPITAL AFFAIR
by Marguerite Lees
Sue Gifford's new job as physiotherapist at a clinic for disabled children seems to clash too often with her boyfriend Keith's needs. And is she imagining that her friendship with Dr Julian Caird has suddenly taken on a new significance?

THE TENDER HEART
by Hazel Fisher
Tender-hearted Nurse Juliet Reed intends devoting her life to caring for the sick. Why then do thoughts of the handsome, brilliant young surgeon Brook Wentworth fill not only her dreams but every waking moment?

SECOND-YEAR LOVE
by Lynne Collins
When Dr Gavin Fletcher advertises his interest in Daisy Palmer by wearing a bunch of her namesake flowers on a ward round the Hartlake Hospital grapevine buzzes with a new romance. But have Daisy's romantic dreams any chance of coming true when Gavin seems to be such a determined bachelor?

On sale where you buy Mills & Boon romances.

The Mills & Boon rose is the rose of romance

How to join in a whole new world of romance

It's very easy to subscribe to the Mills & Boon Reader Service. As a regular reader, you can enjoy a whole range of special benefits. Bargain offers. Big cash savings. Your own free Reader Service newsletter, packed with knitting patterns, recipes, competitions, and exclusive book offers.

We send you the very latest titles each month, postage and packing free – no hidden extra charges. There's absolutely no commitment – you receive books for only as long as you want.

We'll send you details. Simply send the coupon – or drop us a line for details about the Mills & Boon Reader Service Subscription Scheme. Post to: Mills & Boon Reader Service, P.O. Box 236, Thornton Road, Croydon, Surrey CR9 3RU, England. *Please note: READERS IN SOUTH AFRICA please write to: Mills & Boon Reader Service of Southern Africa, Private Bag X3010, Randburg 2125, S. Africa.

Please send me details of the Mills & Boon Subscription Scheme.

NAME (Mrs/Miss) _____ EP3

ADDRESS _____

_____

COUNTY/COUNTRY_____ POST/ZIP CODE_____

BLOCK LETTERS, PLEASE

Mills & Boon
the rose of romance